A Tale Of Two

Ninja Kids

Book 2

The Ancient Protective Stone

By Adam Oakley

COPYRIGHT

ISBN: 978-1-912720-44-6

www.NinjaKidsBook.com

www.InnerPeaceNow.com

www.AdamOakleyBooks.com

Published by Oakhouse Publications.

Oakhouse Publications

Contents

Chapter 1 - The Return 1

Chapter 2 - The Awakening 10

Chapter 3 - Beginning Transcendence 21

Chapter 4 - Meeting Nerris 29

Chapter 5 - Mind Power 43

Chapter 6 - The Tiger Within 52

Chapter 7 - Team Infiltration 68

Chapter 8 - The Overwhelm 79

Chapter 9 - Ascension 87

Chapter 10 - Freedom 97

Chapter 11 - Meeting Aggression 103

Chapter 12 - The Garganfan 112

Chapter 13 - The Spirit Of Darkness 128

Chapter 14 - Demonstralised 139

Chapter 15 - The Navigation Troll 145

Chapter 16 - To Adventure 154

Chapter 17 - The Possession 167

歡
迎

Welcome

Nunchuks

Throwing Darts

Throwing Stars

Daggers

Young Warrior

Ninja Swords

Chapter 1 - The Return

As Martin was being driven home from the airport by his mother, he stared out the window. Things looked normal again. There were long grey roads and lots of cars with people inside of them worrying about so many things. He looked at his mother. She was worrying about something too.

"Mum, what's wrong?" Martin said.

"Nothing," his mother said.

Martin kept looking at her.

"You're worried about something. What is it?"

"How do you know I'm worried? You've never been able to tell before."

"I don't know. I can just tell. You feel nervous. The air feels nervous. What's wrong?"

She was gripping the steering wheel tightly. Her knuckles were turning white.

"I know something has been happening," Martin said. "Kuyasaki told me. Why can't you just tell me?"

"I don't want you to worry."

"Well I'm worrying even more now that you won't tell me. Please, just tell me!"

She explained to him. She explained to him that she was captured by Jacobson Muldridge, the father of the school bully Arthur Muldridge, and that Myasako came to rescue her.

Martin could feel his blood start to boil, but he was relieved to hear what Myasako had done.

"He saved you all by himself?"

"Yes," she said. "Yes he did."

"Does Jacobson still want to come after you?"

"I'm not sure. He just said he was after Myasako, for what he did to Arthur."

"What happened to Arthur?"

"Myasako hurt him very badly. Damaged his insides. He might have broken his leg too. He had to have surgery."

"Cool," Martin said.

"It's not cool, Martin, violence is never the way to solve things."

"Sometimes it is," Martin said. "Sometimes it is, surely Mum?"

His mother went quiet. Now that Myasako was gone, she didn't feel quite so safe.

"I'll protect you Mum, don't worry."

"Did you learn some new things with Kuyasaki?" his mother asked.

"Yes. Yes I did. But there's more I need to learn."

As his mother continued to drive the two of them home, Martin reached inside his pocket, and felt the coldness of the ancient grey stone that Kuyasaki had given him as a gift.

*

In Japan, Myasako was kneeling in front of his father, Kuyasaki, in the dojo. Kuyasaki had just finished explaining what had happened with Myasako's uncle Senzi while Myasako was gone, how Senzi's men captured Martin by accident, mistaking him for Myasako.

"I believe he was seeking a ransom from me. Payment in exchange for your release. He wants to make back the money he lost by selling his shares in our investments too early," Kuyasaki said.

Myasako sat, and listened.

"I feel they will come for you again," Kuyasaki said. "They won't stop. They believe there is money to be made here, but we have a choice."

"What choice?" Myasako asked.

"We either wait for them, alert to every moment, wondering when they might come. Or we go to them directly, and deal with the issue head on."

Myasako was still sitting quietly.

"Let's meet it head on," Myasako said. "Let's go directly to him."

Kuyasaki smiled.

"I'm glad you said that, son," he said.

*

When Martin and his mother arrived home, they saw a man standing in their driveway. It was the middle of the afternoon, and a man was standing there, dressed in black, and he was staring at the both of them, standing in front of the closed garage.

Martin's mother parked in front of him.

"Martin. Do you know that man?" she asked.

"No," Martin said. "Do you?"

"No. Why isn't he moving? He's just standing there. Shall we get out?"

"No. Not yet," Martin said, looking around to see if anyone else was nearby. The streets looked empty.

Martin faced forward to look at the man. The man was looking up at them both, smiling slightly. He looked dirty, unshaven, as if he probably smelt quite bad, and the man turned around and stuck a note on their garage door. He turned back to look at them, and then walked up to Martin's mother's side of the car. He stopped at the window, bent down to look at her, and said through the glass:

"Let me know."

He grinned, and his breath steamed up the window. "I'll be back tomorrow. Let me know," he said again.

He walked off down the street, and Martin and his mother got out of the car.

The two of them walked up to the garage door. They read the note. It said:

"Do you need protective services? I am willing to help you. I heard what happened. My name is Kyle Killen. I'll be back tomorrow."

Martin's mother took the note from the door, looked around at the empty street, and beckoned Martin inside the house.

*

In Japan, Myasako, Kuyasaki and their loyal friend, Takashi, were getting ready to leave the dojo.

"Do you feel fear?" Kuyasaki asked his son.

"No. No yet," Myasako said.

"Remember, if you do, it's okay to feel the fear," Kuyasaki said. "If you embrace it, it will fuel you."

The three of them were placing ropes into their thin cloth bags, tucking nunchuks into their belts, and Myasako saw his father placing daggers into sheaths on the side of his legs.

"Can I take some daggers?" Myasako asked.

Kuyasaki paused, and looked like he was thinking.

"No. You are still too young. If you drop your dagger, it can be used against you, and we want to avoid killing. We do not want to get in trouble with the authorities."

"But we are already breaking into a compound!" Myasako thought. "Please, let me take daggers. Or a sword." Myasako kept his thoughts to himself.

"You know full well that nunchuks can be just as deadly, and you know how to use them well, in a controlled way," Kuyasaki said.

Myasako looked over at Takashi, who was observing a shining, gleaming sword, and putting it into the sheath at his waistline.

Myasako got out his nunchuks, and began practicing, finding a surprising comfort in knowing he would not have to decide what weapon to use, if he ever had to use one tonight.

*

When it was dark, the three ninjas left the dojo.

"It is a three-hour trek to your uncle Senzi's compound," Kuyasaki said, leading the way.

"Can't we just drive?" Myasako said.

Kuyasaki stopped. He looked like he had eaten something bad. He clutched at his stomach.

"How dare you say such a thing? The ninja does not drive to a mission. A road vehicle is far too traceable. It's too loud, we are too vulnerable. There is a method of transportation that I am yet to tell you about. It is dangerous unless you use it properly. Not many people in the world know about it, but it is much faster than walking."

"Well what is it?" Myasako said.

Kuyasaki looked at Takashi. Takashi didn't move a muscle.

"We might need it to escape danger later tonight, so I will show you," Kuyasaki said. "We are moving into the final stages of your training with me. You will now learn the true power of the mind."

The three of them walked off the road, and headed for the Seishin Mountain, far off in the distance.

Spirit

"Sheishin"

Chapter 2 - The Awakening

Martin and his mother were eating dinner in silence.

"Do you think that man will really come back?" Martin said. "I didn't like the look of him."

"Me neither," Martin's mother said. "Although, we could probably use some sort of protection."

Martin took the grey stone out of his pocket and put it on the table. It looked like a large pebble, but every now and then it seemed to give a subtle flash of white.

"Mum, Kuyasaki gave me this," he said.

"Oh, that's nice dear," she said, eating another mouthful of food, wondering if she should call the police again this evening.

"He said it is a protective stone, that it will protect us in any time of danger."

She stopped eating.

"Really?" she said. "How?"

"I don't know. He wouldn't tell me. He said I wouldn't believe him even if he told me. I don't know what it does."

She looked at the stone for a moment.

"Perhaps…oh I don't know, dear, perhaps it's supposed to be more of a mental thing? Like a lucky charm – something that you think might help you, so it makes your mind more positive or something?"

Martin sat back, astonished at her response.

"I don't think so," Martin said. "I think this stone does something. It's not just a normal stone, but I don't think it will do anything until we are in real danger."

"Okay," his mother said, looking worried. "Then we will just have to wait."

That evening, Martin heard his mother on the phone to the police.

"Well what are you doing about it? I've told you what happened! That Jacobson Muldridge took me into his home and held me hostage. I've told you. Have you arrested him yet? What has been done?"

There was a pause.

"Well why haven't you?" she said. "Honestly, he told me he was friendly with the chief of police, but this is just ridiculous! I fear for my life here, we need some protection!"

At that moment, the door knocked.

Martin's mother shouted some more angry words down the phone, then hung up. Martin was at the top of the stairs, looking down at the front door.

It knocked again.

Martin's mother approached the door very quietly. Martin could see she was holding a hammer.

"Don't answer it, Mum," Martin whispered.

She looked up the stairs. She signalled for him to stay there and not move. When she turned towards the door, Martin started to creep down the stairs, the way Kuyasaki had taught him to creep – toes first.

Martin's mother opened the door, very slightly.

"What do you want?" she said.

"I've come back early," said a dark voice. It was the strange man from earlier, Kyle Killen.

"Well go away please," Martin's mother said. She went to close the door, but Kyle jammed his foot in the gap between the frame, and she couldn't shut it.

"No," she said. "No! Go away!"

Kyle forced the door open, shut the door behind him, and grabbed Martin's mother from behind. Martin's pocket started to shake.

"Don't be so rude," Kyle hissed in her ear. "I've been very polite to you, and I want to offer you my services. Both of you."

Martin's leg was now hurting, he grabbed the stone from his pocket where the pain was, took it out and held it out in front of him.

"What's that?" Kyle said. Kyle let go of Martin's mother. "That's a…that's not a…oh no."

Kyle rushed for the door, but it had locked by accident from the inside. He scrambled around, and the stone started to burn Martin's hand, so much that he had to drop it. It bounced on the floor once, and while it was in mid-air after the first bounce, it started to morph into a tiger. The stone exploded, the tiger was full size, about four times the length of Martin's body, and the tiger began to attack and claw at Kyle, who had just managed to get the door open.

Kyle ran away from the house, and the tiger chased him. It bounded up behind him, leapt, took Kyle down and began to slash at Kyle's face.

"Martin? What's happened?" Martin's mother said.

"It's the stone, Mum. It's Kuyasaki's protective stone."

*

Kuyasaki, Myasako and Takashi were walking towards a huge, towering mountain in the distance, across a dry, grassy field. Takashi was constantly scanning their surroundings, holding his sword at his waist with one hand.

"We have never scaled the heights of the Seishin Mountain, because of what dwells within in it," Kuyasaki said. "There is a reason why we have only ever run around the base before."

"What's up there?" Myasako said.

"Many things, many things that people don't dare to talk about. But there is one thing I want to show you today. You will learn how to transport your body to anywhere in the world, in a matter of moments."

"Teleportation?" Myasako said.

"Yes," Kuyasaki said, "but through controlling your own mind, not through the work of some external machine. The mind is the most valuable machinery you could ever have. It creates everything else in your world."

Suddenly the three ninjas heard a rumbling. They felt the rumbling beneath their feet, and they heard the distant sound of old and angry engines coming from behind them. They turned to see three large vans driving across the field towards them.

"It's them. Senzi has sent more men to capture Myasako," Kuyasaki said. "Myasako, run to the mountain."

"But I want to fight!" Myasako said.

"Your time will come, but only when necessary. Do as I say. Run towards the mountain. Go!"

Myasako clenched his fists, wanting to stay and fight, but he followed his father's orders and started running towards the mountain in the distance. As he ran away, he turned to see his father and Takashi begin to run towards the vans. They were sprinting.

Myasako kept running, but watched from a distance as he saw the dots of his father and Takashi take the vans by surprise. No one expects to be attacked while they are trying to chase you down. The men in the van had expected a huge chase to begin with, and now they were on the back foot.

Kuyasaki and Takashi were so fast that they approached the vans before the men knew what to do. The vans stopped, shuddered, and Kuyasaki and Takashi were on them before the men could start pouring out. Kuyasaki and Takashi began to slash at the tyres, Takashi with his sword and Kuyasaki with his daggers, and they disappeared from view behind the back of the vans as Myasako watched while running backwards. There was a pause. Myasako could just see the vans wobbling from side to side. Men in the drivers' seats got out and began to run away, and then the vans stopped wobbling.

Myasako stopped and watched. He had still not reached the mountain.

"I told you to run," said a voice from behind him.

Myasako flinched, ducked and turned, and Kuyasaki and Takashi were both standing there, looking unscathed.

"How did you do that?" Myasako said. "I just saw you down there, in the vans."

"I'll show you," Kuyasaki said. "Come on, let's keep going."

*

Martin and his mother had turned on the news.

"This just in. Reports have been made of a loose tiger running through the streets of Newbevan, a small town in the south of England. Residents have

16

been warned to stay indoors and report any new sightings to the police. The tiger is assumed to be deadly, having already seriously injured one man who is now in hospital."

"Told you, Mum," Martin said.

"Oh, Martin, no one likes to hear that!"

"I did, though. We don't need anyone else, as long as we have that stone."

"Well where is it now? The last we saw was that it morphed into a huge tiger, and started chasing that horrible man down the road. Did you see the blood? It was awful."

"It kept us safe though. That's exactly what Kuyasaki said it would do. Keep us safe. I'm sure it will be back."

Beside the living room where they sat was a large glass door. Martin saw a bird fly down in the evening darkness, and land right outside the door. It began tapping on the door with its beak, hopping around, and tapping again.

"What's that bird doing?" Martin's mother asked.

"It wants to get in," Martin said. "Let's open the door."

"Martin, no, I don't want a little bird in the house, it will be impossible to get it out."

They watched the bird continue to tap, and then when it knew it had their attention it went still, closed itself up, and turned into the small grey stone that Martin had been carrying in his pocket.

"It's the stone! It came back!" Martin said, running over to the door and opening it. He picked up the stone and brought it in the house, locking the door behind him.

"Thank you! Thanks for keeping us safe," Martin said to the cold grey stone. "Can you talk? Can you speak to us? Do you have a name or something?"

The stone remained perfectly still.

"Where are you from? Are you really a stone? Why didn't you kill that man?"

"Martin!" his mother hissed. She didn't like the word 'kill'.

The stone remained silent. Completely silent.

"I don't think it wants to talk," Martin said. "Maybe it only does stuff if we are in danger. Do you fancy going to Jacobson Muldridge's house?"

"Go to bed, Martin," his mother said, with her hand rubbing her forehead. "Please."

守護者

Guardian

Chapter 3 - Beginning Transcendence

"This is what so much of your training has been leading to," Kuyasaki said to his son. "Transcendence of the physical. Your body is strong, and so is your mind. All of those hours spent in meditation have led to your clarity. And now you can begin to move beyond what people think is possible."

"But how is it possible?" Myasako said. He couldn't understand what his father and Takashi had just done to appear behind him so quickly.

"Anything is possible," Kuyasaki said, "but doubt will prevent it from happening. Our assumptions about the human body are often false. We limit the body to how we perceive it with our eyes – a lump of flesh without any extraordinary abilities. We only have to inspect our bodies to see that it turns water and food into a living being. That is a miracle in itself."

Myasako's question had still not been answered.

"You know from your training that the mind can influence the body," Kuyasaki continued. "You know that the two can become one. You know that with your mind you can ease pain, speed up the healing process, even a lighter mood will allow more energy to flow through you. The mind can influence the body. A free mind can be free with its abilities."

"I'm not sure if I can do it," Myasako said.

"What have I taught you before!" Kuyasaki scolded him as they approached the base of the mountain. "I have done my best to keep you away from all limiting beliefs, self-doubt and mis-education about the power of the body and mind. But still the society infiltrates your system with immediate doubt. What is the use in doubt, if we are going to try it anyway? Why not be free while you engage in an activity? Doubt pulls you away from the task and steals your energy, focusing on an outcome you don't want. Things are more difficult if we believe them to be difficult. Now come on."

Kuyasaki began to climb the rocks of the mountain. The gradient was not too steep and Myasako began to follow after him, with Takashi still constantly scanning their surroundings, and following after the both of them.

*

Later that night, Martin was woken up by a noise. He looked over to his right, and the little grey stone was moving, by itself. It was shaking on his desk.

"Are we in danger?" Martin said out loud, sitting up quickly.

Then the stone stopped moving, for a moment it was still. Then it fell down to the floor, disappeared from Martin's view, and up stood Kuyasaki, standing there in front of Martin.

"Kuyasaki?" Martin said.

"No," the man said. "I am only taking the form of someone you trust. You do not seem to trust many people. Where is your father?"

"He went away, a long time ago," Martin said. He wanted to change the subject. "So you are the stone?"

"Yes. Some know me as the Protostone. Others see me as just a pebble. I can take any form I wish, for the purpose of keeping my owner safe."

"And I am your owner?" Martin asked.

"For now, yes," the man said.

Martin stared at the man. It looked exactly like Kuyasaki. It sounded exactly like him.

"So what now?" Martin said. "Are we in danger right now?"

"Not right now, no. But generally, yes. I sense that Jacobson Muldridge is assembling more men, and developing a plan to get revenge on you and your mother, for what Myasako did to him and his son.

He feels embarrassed. He wants the moral victory. He wants to cause pain."

"Well how can we stop him?"

The form of Kuyasaki went quiet.

"I'm not sure," he said. "But I need to take extra protective measures. I will give you something. This is not normally allowed, but since these are quite severe circumstances, it is my nature to transmit some properties directly to you, for safety reasons. You may choose to have the characteristics of any animal, all while keeping your human form. Choose wisely."

"Any animal?" Martin said. He looked at his bedsheets as he was thinking.

"So if I chose a bird, I could fly, if I chose an elephant, I would have strength. If I chose a tiger…"

Martin was imagining all the traits a tiger would have for fighting. He remembered what the stone had done to Kyle Killen as a tiger. It had speed, strength, agility, stealth, ferociousness…a tiger could protect his mother better than any other creature he could think of.

"Tiger. I choose a tiger."

"You must be careful," the stone said. "The more destructive the animal, the more difficult the traits will be to control. Your mind might not be strong enough to…"

"Tiger," Martin said. "If it becomes too much for me, you can always take it away, can't you?"

"Yes," the stone said, "but only if you ask…"

"I choose the tiger," Martin said, lost in his enthusiasm. He always wanted to feel what it would be like to be a tiger, to have that amount of power…

"Tiger! Tiger! Tiger!"

"Very well," the stone said. "But you must not let it take over you under normal circumstances. Only when you are threatened should you release the tiger within. I would not permit this unless I feared such an intensive attack from a man who can even influence the police."

"Good, good," Martin said, still excited. "So give me the tiger. Give me the inner tiger."

"Actually, you already have it," the stone said. "I will just wake it up. I will disappear and resume my dormant form now. As long as you are within sight of me, you will have access to the powers of the tiger. I will also awaken from sleep if ever I am needed. Put me back on the desk."

The form of Kuyasaki vanished, as if turning into a light dust, and Martin picked up the stone to put back on the desk.

As he touched the stone he felt a huge roar of a tiger fill his mind, surround his body, and then subside into nothing. He put the stone on the desk, and felt himself lazily falling to sleep, like a big cat lying in the shade.

*

The next morning, Martin walked down the stairs.

"Hi Mum," he said. He spotted a bird on the grass outside. Martin instantly crouched down low and stopped moving.

"Martin, what are you doing?"

Martin snapped out of it. He forgot that he had just wanted to eat that bird.

"I've been thinking, we should go away for a while," his mother said. "Your school holidays have just begun. We can go and stay with your aunt Nerris."

"Oh, not aunt Nerris," Martin said. "No Mum, do we really have to run away?"

"At the moment we do, yes. It's not safe for us here, even with that stone of yours. Has it done anything else since the tiger incident last night?"

"Um…no," Martin said. He didn't want to worry her, he didn't want to have to explain that he had chosen to awaken his inner tiger, even though he might not yet be ready. He lay down in the middle of the kitchen and started to stretch his body out.

"Martin, please not in here. Pack your things, we're leaving soon."

Power

Chapter 4 - Meeting Nerris

A few miles away, at the top of the hill overlooking the town, Jacobson Muldridge was in a large underground room, with three men wearing lab coats, who were all inspecting screens. One of the screens was showing a bird's-eye view of some houses. Jacobson had cameras everywhere.

"Sir, I think they are leaving," one of the men in lab coats said.

"Yes sir, they have luggage. They must be leaving town," another man said.

"Fine," Jacobson said. "Maybe we can capture them in transit if we can steer them in the right direction. Do we still have control of the traffic lights?"

"Yes sir, but I can only hang on for a few more minutes."

"Have Vehicle One follow her. Create a diversion before she leaves town, have her break down beside the Anglesey meadow. It's usually deserted. Did you attach the engine disruptor to her car?"

"Yes, sir. It's fully installed."

They watched as Martin and his mother walked out of their home, locked the door behind them and got into their little blue car.

"What's that? Is that a monkey?" Jacobson said.

The lab assistant zoomed in closer with the camera. There seemed to be a small monkey climbing out of Martin's pocket, clambering its way underneath the car.

"What on earth is a monkey doing in his pocket? What is it doing?"

"We can't see, sir."

A few moments later, the monkey reappeared, and climbed back inside the car. It was holding a small grey casing, and it threw the casing on the lawn.

"Litterbug," Jacobson said.

"Sir, that looks like our engine disruptor."

"What! Oh for goodness' sake, how did it know it was there? Is it a mechanic? Were you seen in the night when you planted it?"

"Sir, we did our best not to be detected."

"Oh, you fools. Follow them anyway. Just Vehicle One. And find out where he got a monkey from."

They all watched as Martin's mother started the engine and began to drive away, with Martin and the monkey sitting in the back.

"I've always hated monkeys," Jacobson said.

The blue car made its way down the road. A large black SUV followed behind them in the distance. The blue car stopped at some traffic lights.

"Give them a slow puncture," Jacobson said. "While they are stopped."

One of the lab assistants began typing furiously. The black SUV pulled up behind the blue car, and a large man dressed in black got out. He approached the blue car casually, and began to reach inside his back pocket for something. Suddenly the window of the blue car opened, and the same monkey jumped out. It looked at the man, jumped up and clamped on to the man's face. The man started flailing around.

A noise came through the speakers beside Jacobson.

"Please advise! Please advise! There is an attack a...a monkey attack! Please advise!"

Jacobson reached over to the microphone, and pushed the button to speak.

"Destroy that stupid monkey! Destroy it!"

The first man outside fell to the ground. He was no longer breathing. An armed man stepped out of the driver's seat of the black SUV, and before he could raise his weapon to fire, the monkey screamed, bared its fangs, and leapt straight at the man's neck. Jacobson watched as his best guard fell to the ground, dropped his weapon, and lay there, bleeding, while the monkey hopped off and jumped back in the blue car.

It began to drive away.

"That's it," Jacobson said. "Now they've really made me angry."

*

When the monkey jumped back inside the car after taking down those two men, it turned back into a stone.

Martin's mother started driving quickly.

"They must be following us. They must be watching us all the time!" she said. "There's no use in us even running! They know exactly where we'll be!"

"Calm down, Mum, calm down, we'll be okay."

"How? How will we be? We can't keep running forever, Martin, and one monkey or one tiger can only hold back so many men. They will come for us all at once, all together, and we won't be able to stop them!"

"Well what about Nerris? Just before we left the house you told me that she had an idea, but she didn't tell you what it is."

"Oh you know your aunt Nerris. She always has these crazy ideas, and none of them ever work out properly. Her inventions always break. She's not even completely safe to be around, but it's all the family I have. You know what she's like. You never liked going round there."

"Only because of the smell. She's always inventing something in her basement, and it always makes the place stink. I don't mind Nerris. She's nice enough. Just a bit…different."

"Yeh. That's one word for it," Martin's mother said. "Well let's just hope that whatever idea she has, will actually work this time. In twenty years of inventing, she's bound to find something that works. Isn't she?"

"Hope so," Martin said, stroking the grey stone with his finger. "Hope so."

*

They arrived at Nerris's house. It was a house that looked as if it was falling apart. The other houses on the road looked nicer, more stable. Nerris's looked neglected. And it was, because all Nerris did was spend time in her basement, out of sight.

Martin and his mother got out of the car and looked around. They couldn't see anyone following them. They hurried up the little path that was overgrown with grass and plants and flowers from the little front garden that was now a meadow. Martin's mother knocked on the door.

The grass was up to Martin's waist, leaning against him.

"Hang on!" they heard an old, grating voice call from downstairs. They heard clunking, swearing, and some footsteps plonking up the stairs.

The plonking stopped.

"Who is it?" the voice said aggressively.

"Nerris it's us."

"Are you alone? What's the secret password for safety?"

Martin's mother sighed.

"Merry Merry, let's be Merry," she said.

The door was being unlocked, unbolted, unchained, many times all the way down the door until it opened, and the hunched-over, dirty-faced figure of

Nerris was standing there, poking her head around the door.

"Get in! Get in you two!" she said, hurrying them in with her hand.

Martin could smell a heavy smell again. It smelt metallic.

"Put these on," Nerris said.

She handed them both white masks to put over their faces. She had just been working on something.

"Where's yours?" Martin asked.

"I'm used to it, love. Don't worry about me. Come on, no time to waste."

Martin and his mother put their bags down on the old carpet, and followed a trundling Nerris down the stairs, into the dark basement.

When they reached the bottom, Nerris was standing there behind a workbench. On the workbench was a huge grey gun, looking like it had been made of trash can lids and belt buckles.

"Here it is," she said, beaming with a smile. Her teeth looked grey, but her eyes were bright. She was wearing a large brown poncho. She always seemed to be wearing it whenever Martin saw her.

"Nerris, that's not safe," Martin's mother said, backing away.

"It is. It is!" Nerris said. "I've tested it! I've tested it many times. Many many times!"

"What does it do?" Martin said. "Kill people?"

Nerris burst into laughter. She threw her head back and closed her bright eyes.

"No lad no! Of course not. I mean, it could…I would have to spend another day working on it, but no, this is what I call the Demonstraliser."

"What does it do then?" Martin asked again, starting to approach it. His mother grabbed him by the shoulder to stop him.

"You point it at anything that is being a monster, anything that is being aggressive. When the beam hits them, they forget why they were ever so angry. Anyone who comes after you, we'll shoot them with this, and they'll go back to being sane again. It works a treat."

"So you've tried it before on people?" Martin asked.

"But there's just one catch," Nerris said, ignoring his question. "If you shoot someone who is not coming after you, it might have the opposite effect. I haven't tested that part. If you shoot a calm, kind person, they might turn into a monster. I'm not sure. So you have to watch your aim, and that's not what I've perfected just yet. It has quite a kick to it, this thing."

She tapped the weapon, proudly admiring it with her bright eyes.

"Plus you've gotta be careful firing it! It takes a while to recharge itself at the moment, but charges much faster when it's in contact with the earth."

Nerris looked at Martin's mother. She looked tired.

"Don't worry," Nerris said. "I'm up all night anyway. You two get some rest. I'll stand guard, make sure no monsters come for ya! But we'll have to get to the source at some point. We'll have to go right up to him and shoot that Muldridge fella, and turn him sane again."

Martin's stomach started to grumble.

"Hungry, lad?" Nerris said. Strangely enough, while most of her house was a mess, Nerris's kitchen was always spotless, and she cooked wonderful food. Sometimes it was so good, it unsettled Martin.

"Yeh, I am. Do you have any antelope?" Martin asked.

"Sorry, love?"

"Antelope. No? What about bison? Any bison around here we could catch?"

"No, love, no. Got chicken. That's about it. Will you eat a chicken?"

Nerris started walking past them, back up the stairs to get the food ready.

"Yeh, thanks," Martin said. "You don't even have to cook it, I'll just eat it as it is."

"That's not a good idea, but I like your style," Nerris said.

Martin's mother watched him walk up the stairs, and noticed that when he was nearly at the top, he started to walk on all fours.

*

Later that evening, Jacobson Muldridge and his son, Arthur, were at the dinner table. Arthur still had a large bandage around his stomach from his operation, after Myasako had kicked him at school. He had been advised to eat less than usual, but he was eating just as much.

"Dad, when will Uncle Kyle get out of hospital?"

"I'm not sure, boy," Jacobson said, cutting through a piece of steak on his plate.

"Have they caught the tiger yet?"

"No, not yet."

"Hmm," Arthur said.

"What? Out with it, Arthur," Jacobson said.

"Well Dad, do you think *they* had something to do with it? I know the hospital says Kyle is delirious from his painkillers, but maybe what Kyle said was true – that Martin had some kind of stone, a stone that Kyle recognised, and when that stone senses danger, it creates an animal to protect the owner. Could that be possible?"

Jacobson stopped eating. Arthur carried on.

"Any animal? It could form any animal?" Jacobson said, wiping his mouth.

"That's what Uncle Kyle said. Weren't you listening?"

Arthur was shovelling mashed potatoes down his throat. Jacobson began to stare at the ceiling. He started to think out loud.

"I didn't think it would ever be possible," Jacobson said, "but maybe…maybe it is true. Today, we were watching them, they had a monkey in the car…"

"A monkey?" Arthur said. "I want a monkey too, Dad, why do they get a monkey but not me?"

"Quiet, Arthur. Don't you realise? That might be from their stone that Kyle was talking about. It's not a pet. And you know why you can't have a monkey. I don't like them."

"You're scared of them," Arthur said, smashing his peas with his fork on the table, making them go everywhere.

"I'm not scared!" Jacobson snapped across the table. "I just don't like them. I don't like them at all. They can't be trusted. They are just like people."

Arthur took some pills from his pocket. He put one in his mouth.

"You better not take more than one this time," his father said. "You know what happened last time. You said you had terrible nightmares when you took too much of your medication. You were practically in a coma for days."

"Oh, leave me alone," Arthur said, embarrassed from his overdose. "The nightmares weren't that bad."

"How did you even get hold of them? The nurse is supposed to keep them from you. They can be dangerous."

"I keep taking the bottle from her," Arthur said. "She keeps leaving them on my pillow by accident!

Silly nurse. She always tells me not to take more than one, just like you."

Jacobson thought about his son's welfare for a second longer, and then his mind switched to the possibility of a magical stone, that he might be able to steal…

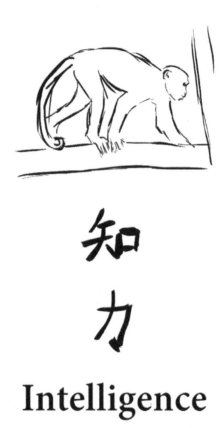

知
力

Intelligence

Chapter 5 - Mind Power

The climb was long. As Kuyasaki, Myasako and Takashi scaled the mountain, one after the other, they passed dark caves that Myasako could sense things living within.

"Don't look into any of those caves," Kuyasaki said, as they passed them. "We are only focussed on one today."

After walking for a while, the mountain started to become steeper.

"We have to climb here," Kuyasaki said. "Watch your step. Make sure you are on secure ground before you move again."

Myasako grabbed hold of little ledges and jagged pieces of rock that were sticking out of the mountain. They climbed vertically for a while, and then made it on to a ledge.

"Here we are," Kuyasaki said. "This is the cave. This is the cave of transportation."

"Why have I never known about this?" Myasako said.

"Because it can be dangerous. You need an experienced supervisor. If you walked into that cave, not knowing what to expect, you might end up lost in another dimension altogether. Come. Follow me."

Takashi climbed up behind them, and followed the two into the cave, looking behind him as he walked.

The cave was dark and moist. Myasako could hear dripping coming from somewhere. Ahead of them they could see a green pool of water. It was a shining bright green, and the smell was strong, but Myasako didn't recognise it. It smelt like a fresh woodland, but much more intense.

"What's that smell?" Myasako said.

"It's the water. There will come a day when you no longer need the water to transport yourself. You will be able to do it from anywhere. But to begin with, the water is needed."

"What do we do?"

"You visualise where you want to go. I have told you before what your uncle Senzi's compound looks like. If you hold the intention of going to Uncle Senzi's compound, to a specific area of the compound, then you will end up there. But you must make the image in your mind strong and constant. If it changes while you are in transit, you might end up somewhere else. Where you want to go must be your dominant vibration, the dominant feeling that you hold. You must feel what it's like to be there. See the surroundings in your mind, see yourself in the exact position you want to go to."

"And where exactly do we want to end up?" Myasako asked.

"In the dungeon," Kuyasaki said. "He has a dungeon where he keeps some of his workers. He calls them workers. Really they are slaves. We will not be detected there. The guards remain above ground, and many of the slaves will be working elsewhere."

"How do you know this?" Myasako said. "Have you ever been?"

"Not physically," Kuyasaki said. "But I have seen it. Parts of his compound are clear to me, others are not. Travelling without the body is a whole other exercise that we are yet to cover. Right now we need our bodies to confront your uncle and stop him from coming after you."

"Wouldn't it be better to do this at night?" Myasako asked.

"No. Senzi is even more paranoid at night. He increases his security, and we have no time to spare. He might even come again for you in the night. We can not wait for him."

Myasako looked into the green pool of water.

"Now," Kuyasaki said. "The dungeon is dark and brown, very much like this cave, but with a foul and stuffy smell. It smells...you can imagine how it smells, if his slaves are spending the entire night and evening in their cages."

"Will we set them free?" Myasako said.

"We will have to see," Kuyasaki said. "Some might not want to be set free. The world can be a challenging place for those who have no experience of it. We will see. Now. Visualise yourself there. See yourself there. Are you able to?"

"Yes," Myasako said. "I can see it very clearly."

"Good. Now hold it, and jump into the water. I will go first. Then you, then Takashi. Just hold on to your vision. Ready?"

"Yes."

Kuyasaki put on his black ninja mask, closed his eyes, jumped into the water, and disappeared. The water flashed an intense green light.

"Go," Takashi said from behind Myasako. Myasako put on his own mask, held on to his vision, and jumped in.

As he jumped, Myasako had a fearful thought:

"How will we get back?"

He landed in the water, and the entire world seemed to turn green. His body became formless.

The fear voiced itself again:

"Will we ever make it back?"

The world lost its greenness, and Myasako emerged out of the water. He was back in the cave. Now he was alone. Takashi was gone.

Myasako could normally deal with fearful thoughts, but this one had lived in him for too long. It had masked the vision of where he needed to be. He needed to trust his father. He knew he could trust his father.

He closed his eyes again, saw himself appearing in the dungeon beside his father and Takashi, and he jumped.

The water splashed, the world went green, and he held his vision. He was in the dungeon, he could see and feel himself in the dungeon.

And then the swirling greens that surrounded him began to take shape. They began to form the walls of a dungeon. Myasako intensified his vision, and within a blink of an eye, Myasako landed on the ground, beside Kuyasaki and Takashi.

"I knew you could do it," Kuyasaki said. "What happened?"

"I thought about coming back, so I ended up back in the cave."

"Okay," Kuyasaki said. "There are far more dangerous scenarios you could have imagined, and you did well to fix your mind on where you wanted to be. Well done."

Myasako looked around. They were in a dark corner of the dungeon. They could see cages on either side, with some people lying inside of them, dirty-looking people with rags for clothes, who had not even noticed the three ninjas were there. Most of the cages were empty.

"We must move in silence," Kuyasaki whispered. "Follow me."

The three ninjas began to move swiftly, silently, past the few sleeping people in empty cages, who had not yet been woken up by any sound...

*

In the main dining hall of the compound, Myasako's uncle Senzi was sitting, devouring a chicken. He was alone. His assistant entered. His assistant was a thin man who was always made to wear the same black and red uniform.

Senzi wore an eyepatch over one eye, a squint in the other, and he had a deadly look on his face.

Senzi's assistant reported what had just come through the phone. The capture of Myasako was not a success.

Senzi listened to his assistant explain what happened, and his chin started to wobble with fury. He had grown more round over the years, since he parted ways with Kuyasaki.

"Gone? What? What do you mean they are gone? Where did they go?"

"The men don't know, sir. They said they woke up in their van, and the two ninjas were gone, along with the boy. They were headed for the Seishin Mountain."

"Well why didn't they follow them up the mountain?"

"There are stories about that mountain, sir. Many of the men were too afraid..."

"Well what am I paying them for?! If those three were headed for the Seishin Mountain...they could be planning anything. They could be here right now..."

"Sir, I very much doubt that."

Senzi threw down his chicken on the plate.

"Well what do you know? You don't know Kuyasaki like I do. I thought three vanloads of armed men would have been enough. We even gave them each a gun! Kuyasaki has very little experience dealing with guns! How could they have taken out three vanloads of men?"

"They say they caught them off guard..."

Senzi stood to his feet.

"Increase security. Something tells me they are coming for me now. Switch on the night alarms early. If anything moves around the walls of this compound, I want to know about it. Take me to the vault."

"Sir, they couldn't possibly intrude on us. This place is a fortress..."

"Don't tell me what's possible or not. It's three ninjas we are dealing with. We've failed to catch them off guard, and a ninja is at his most deadly when he's the one doing the sneaking! Now take me to the vault. And bring my chicken."

"Yes, sir." His assistant ran over to the table, grabbed the plate of food, and followed his master out of the main hall.

Mind

Chapter 6 - The Tiger Within

"There's something different about you, Martin," Nerris said, as the three of them were eating dinner. The table was clean, but on the floor surrounding them there were hundreds of pieces of metal and wire that Nerris could use for her inventions.

"Yes," Martin's mother said. "Martin, use your knife and fork."

Martin was snarling as he bit into his food. He was tearing at flesh and licking his plate. He snapped out of it.

"Oh yeh, sorry Mum," he said.

Nerris stared at him.

"Hang on," she said. She got up, left the table and went towards the basement. She disappeared. A few moments later she was back, with a little hand-held device with a red light on the end.

She pointed it at Martin, and the little machine started beeping.

"What's that, Nerris?" Martin's mother said.

"I don't believe it," Nerris said. She sat back down and put her device on the table. It was flashing red.

"Why didn't you tell me?" she said to the both of them.

"What?" Martin asked.

"Something has happened to you. You've taken on something else's energy. You aren't all human at the moment."

"What do you mean?" Martin's mother said. "Martin? What does she mean? And what is that little machine, Nerris?"

"It's a purity detector. I made it years ago for someone who wanted to test whether their dog was really a pure breed."

"Martin?" his mother asked.

Martin put down his knife and fork. He had flashes in his mind of wanting to leap over the table and...

"It's nothing," Martin said. "The stone, it gave me something. It gave me extra protection, just in case."

"What stone?" Nerris said, leaning forward, intrigued.

"I have a magic stone," Martin said. He got it out and put it on the table. "It gave me some extra qualities, of a tiger."

Nerris got up and walked around the table to pick up the stone. She picked it up.

"I don't believe it. I didn't know these were real!" she said. "Can I test it? Can I take it down to the basement?"

"No," Martin said. "It's a living thing. Don't, Nerris."

Nerris reluctantly put it back down on the table.

"So it gave you some extra powers?" Martin's mother asked.

"Kind of," Martin said. "I'm more like a tiger now, so if any more men come and I have to fight them off, I can fight like a tiger. I think I've got it under control."

Martin saw that a few birds landed in Nerris's garden. He shot up, ran to the back door, opened it, and leapt at the birds. They all flew away.

"Ah, damn," Martin said. "I might wait out here, quietly, until they come back. Thanks for the meal, Nerris, it was great."

"Okay, love," she said.

*

"Nerris, you need to take it out of him. What if he starts to believe he's actually a tiger? What if I lose him altogether? I knew that stone was no good, I knew it."

Nerris and Martin's mother were in the basement.

"It *is* good," Nerris said. "I have heard legends about the stone. It will fight fiercely for whoever owns it. It puts safety over everything else, though. It's designed to have Martin survive at all costs. It would rather have him believing he's a tiger and be safe, than believing he's a boy and fall into the hands of someone evil. It's just doing its job."

"But we don't need him to be a tiger! We've already got the stone, your Demonstraliser. We have enough, don't we?"

"Let's give it one more day," Nerris said. "If they don't come tonight, then I can extract the tiger properties tomorrow."

"How?"

"I have something I made a few years ago. Again, it was for dogs, for making their DNA pure for breeding, but I stopped letting people use it when I realised it wasn't fair on the dogs."

"So...it won't turn Martin into a dog?"

Nerris burst out laughing, then she stopped to think about it.

"Well, hopefully not, Amanda. Hopefully not."

*

That night, the stone beside Martin's bed started shaking again. It woke him up.

"What?" Martin asked, sitting bolt upright.

The stone turned into a small monkey again, and it was tapping on the bedroom window, asking for it to be opened. Martin reached up, grabbed the handle, and pushed open the window. The monkey jumped out, and Martin saw it land on the ground, and run off down the road.

*

"A dragon!" Jacobson yelled. "A dragon!"

He and his three assistants watched from the screens in their underground lair, as they saw five SUVs full of armed guards being torched by the fiery breath of a dragon in the middle of the road. The men were jumping out of the vehicles and running away, and Jacobson's cameras could see it all.

"Sir, we should stop pursuing this. This is becoming far too dangerous."

"No. I need that stone more than anything else now. I don't care about the boy or the woman. I

56

just want the stone. Who cares about the boy? Once he's back at school, Arthur can start bullying him again, and the woman...well, she never did anything. It was Myasako I really wanted, and now he's gone. Now there's the stone. All of this wanting for revenge has led me towards this stone. Abort all plans of capture. Now let's look into how we can acquire this stone."

One of the assistants spoke into the microphone in front of his face. He pushed a button underneath the microphone to speak.

"Operation terminated. We are no longer seeking to harm or capture anyone."

As soon as he said that, the dragon disappeared, and Jacobson could see a little monkey running away, down the road, back into the house that looked much more run-down than the rest.

*

The news was on again the next day. Nerris didn't have a television. Martin's mother was watching it on her phone.

"Local residents yesterday spotted what appeared to be a dragon torching numerous SUVs. Images have been captured, and videos were taken. Viewer discretion is advised. The following footage contains some upsetting scenes."

Martin's mother watched as carloads of men were torched with fire from a huge dragon standing in the middle of the road. She watched through squinted eyes, but noticed that none were being harmed. By the time the cars were engulfed in their own flames, the men had escaped and were running away down the road.

Nerris walked in. Sometimes she slept outside.

"Oh, no not the news," she said. "Turn that off. All they want to do is make you feel bad."

"Look," Martin's mother said, showing her the phone.

Nerris shut her eyes tight to not see. When she heard the word 'dragon' being said, she opened her bright eyes, and watched.

"That's just down the road," Nerris said. "So the stone did its job."

"Someone saw the monkey run towards this house," Martin's mother said.

At the back door, at that very moment, appeared three people dressed in police uniforms. One was a woman. Two were large men standing behind her. They were holding a search warrant. They knocked on the door.

"One moment please!" Nerris called to them. She turned and ran upstairs. She burst into Martin's room.

"Martin follow me, quick. Grab the stone."

Martin was still in his pyjamas. He grabbed the stone and followed Nerris downstairs.

"Hide in the basement! Quick!" she hissed.

Martin went down the stairs, grabbed a mask hanging on the wall, and stood at the bottom of the basement. He looked up and saw Nerris typing a number into a keypad on the wall, and then shut the door behind her.

Then it all went completely quiet.

"Sorry about that," Nerris said, opening the back door to the police. "I wasn't quite presentable." Her hair was a mess, and she still had a dirty-looking brown poncho on. She stank of metal, and the smell made the police officers recoil.

"We have a warrant, madam, to search your home for any evidence of..." the female officer read the writing on the warrant out loud; "Stones or transforming creatures."

Nerris looked puzzled. "Really? Okay. Why?"

"Madam, please let us in or we will have to use force."

"Okay," she said. "Come in."

Nerris stood aside, and the police officers entered. Their feet were surrounded by metal and wires.

"Is there a child here?" the policewoman said.

"No," Nerris said.

"Who are you?" the policewoman asked Martin's mother.

Nerris shook her head violently from behind the police officers, looking at Martin's mother.

"She doesn't speak," Nerris said. "She's my sister. She had a recent traumatic event and has lost the ability to speak. She's seeing someone about it."

The policewoman stared at Martin's mother. Then she moved on.

"Do you have a basement?" the policewomen asked. The policemen were turning over old bits of wire and metal on the floor, wearing gloves, looking for a stone.

"Yes, yes I do," Nerris said. "It's just around the corner there. Just open the door."

Martin's mother was squirming and thrashing inside. They were going to find Martin and the stone!

The policewoman opened the door and began walking downstairs. Nerris looked over at Martin's mother, and winked.

Five minutes later the policewoman appeared.

"Okay," she said. "Thank you. Any luck here?" she asked the two policemen. They shook their heads to say no.

"We were told that there is a boy staying here. The son of Amanda Davies."

"He's not here," Nerris said. "He didn't tell us where he was going."

The policewoman stared at her.

"When will he be back?"

"No idea."

There was a pause.

"We will be here a while longer," the policewoman said. "We still have to search upstairs."

"Take your time," Nerris said. "Cup of tea?"

*

When the police officers had left, Nerris opened the door to the basement. She typed a number into the keypad on the wall, closed the door, then opened it again.

"Come up now, Martin, it's safe."

Martin bounded and leapt up the stairs.

"What was all that about?" he said. "I couldn't hear a thing."

Martin's mother stood up. "What did you do, Nerris? Did you hide Martin?"

"Sort of," she said. "I have an alternative basement. A normal one, with nothing in it. She went down that one instead."

"How come all of a sudden your inventions seem to be working?" Amanda said, walking up to Martin to put her arm around him. "They used to always fail when we were younger."

"Persistence," Nerris said, sitting on the sofa and putting her feet up on the coffee table. "Persistence is the key, my dear. Now tell Martin what just happened, please. I need to think."

*

"What did they find? Did those fools really believe they were police officers?" Jacobson said that evening. He was back in his lair with his assistants.

There was silence.

"Nothing, sir. They found nothing inside," one of them said.

"What? Nothing? What about the boy?"

"No. Just his mother, and who we believe to be his aunt."

"And after questioning?"

"They denied knowledge of anything. The mother would not speak. Apparently she is traumatised."

"Right," Jacobson said, scratching his chin. "They can always see us coming. We are going to have to play the long game."

"Yes, sir."

"You know what to do."

"Yes, sir, of course."

Jacobson left the lair, and went up the stairs. He fancied a walk, and wanted time to imagine how great it would be when he would finally get a hold of that magical stone.

"Prepare a letter of apology, and a cheque," he said as he left.

"For how much, sir?"

"One million pounds."

*

A few days later, a letter came in through the letterbox. Nerris waddled over, picked it up and looked at it.

"Amanda! Letter here for you," she called. "It feels, it feels big, but it's only small. Look at the fancy writing on the front."

Amanda walked over and took the letter. There was something slimy about the handwriting, something slanting and slimy and unpleasant.

She opened the envelope. Inside there was a letter, and a cheque. She looked at the cheque first, and gasped. Then she read the letter.

Dearest Amanda,

I'm writing to apologise to you, to your family, and to the young Japanese boy. I have been a menace, an unwelcome, unfair menace, and I am writing to also say that I will now leave you alone. It is clear that chasing down you and your son in vengeance for what happened to Arthur results in nothing but danger for my own men, and I will stop from here on in. I'm sorry. Please accept this cheque as an apology for what I have put you and your family through.

With best wishes,

Jacobson Muldridge.

Amanda showed Nerris the cheque. Nerris quivered slightly.

"Do you know what we could do with this?" Nerris said. "Do you know what I could invent with that kind of money?"

"We aren't taking it," Amanda said, snatching back the cheque. "I don't believe him for one moment. One million is like pocket change for him, it doesn't mean anything. If we cash it...I don't know...I don't want anything to do with him at all. But perhaps we could show this to the police as evidence?"

Nerris sighed and sat down on the sofa.

"He is too friendly with people high up in the police force," Nerris said. "It would probably disappear. I used to know a few policemen who realised what was happening high up in the ranks. They saw the corruption and broke away to do their own policing. A group of vigilantes they were, good honest people who just wanted to protect the community. You have to remember that, Martin. Not all police are affected by corruption. Some are good."

"Okay," Martin said. He walked in and began stretching himself out on the floor, like a cat.

"Now," Nerris said, "can we discuss whether you still want to be gradually taken over by a tiger from the inside, or not?"

弁護人

Defender

Chapter 7 - Team Infiltration

Kuyasaki, Myasako and Takashi were ascending the stairs, leaving the dungeon. The stairs were cold and stony, and Myasako could feel the jagged edges of them digging in through his thin ninja shoes.

There was a door at the top of the stairs. Kuyasaki stopped, and gave a hand signal for the other two to stop.

They could hear people walking past outside the door.

When it became absolutely silent, Kuyasaki slowly opened the door and peered around. He flowed out of the door, Myasako followed, and Takashi closed the door silently as the three of them walked into an empty corridor.

Kuyasaki led the way, staying close to the wall. Myasako had never seen his father on a real mission before. He looked almost ethereal, as if beneath the black ninja suit, nobody was there.

They reached the end of the corridor, where another one intersected. They could hear footsteps coming. It was the voice of Senzi's assistant. The footsteps stopped. Senzi's assistant began speaking to someone.

"He's convinced they are coming here," the assistant muttered. "He wants all the guards out. Wake up every guard who would normally be doing the night shift. We'll bring more in for later this evening."

"Yes, sir," came a burly voice.

"He's in his chamber now. The code has changed again. It's 43961."

"Yes, sir."

"Now go and get the guards. Come to his room when you're done and type in the code."

"Yes, sir."

"Well go on then."

The three ninjas heard a pair of heavy boots running towards them from around the corner. All three became perfectly still.

The guard turned the corner and ran past them, as if they were not there.

The guard continued running, off and away down the corridor.

Myasako had no idea how the guard hadn't seen them. He wanted to ask, but knew he could not make a sound.

Kuyasaki began to follow Senzi's assistant through the compound. Myasako and Takashi followed after. Takashi was constantly looking behind them.

Kuyasaki would wait to turn corners until he felt the coast was clear, then would silently sprint through spaces, with Myasako doing well to keep up. Then they approached the house kitchen.

Around another corner, Kuyasaki watched as kitchen staff walked in and out of the kitchen, carrying hot plates of food.

"Haven't the trainees been fed yet!" Senzi's assistant screamed. "They should have been fed an hour ago. We need them on patrol."

Kitchen staff were scurrying past the little man, avoiding his eye contact.

"Someone answer me. Chef!"

Soon a large, fat, tired, sweating chef appeared at the door of the kitchen, and looked down on the little man.

The chef listened to some of the assistant's screams, and began to look as if he was boiling from within.

He picked up the assistant and pinned him against the wall.

The chef began to whisper something ferocious in the assistant's ear.

Kuyasaki saw an opportunity. Across from them was a door. Kuyasaki skipped across the corridor, opened the door, and lying on the floor was a young girl, asleep. She was at the foot of the staircase.

Kuyasaki hopped over her silently. Myasako looked at her. She was his age, dressed in black, with a sword at her waist. Myasako hopped over her too, followed by Takashi. They made no sound. The three of them ran up the stairs, the endless stairs, until they reached a very large bedroom.

"This is Senzi's room," Kuyasaki whispered. "He likes to be near the kitchen."

"Who was that girl?" Myasako said.

"That's his main guard," Kuyasaki said. "But he never gives her any rest. Ever."

They were in a grand bedroom. The bed was huge with golden posts at all four corners. The rug looked like it was made from the skin of a tiger, with the head and teeth at the front, and Myasako started to feel fury inside of him at the thought of a tiger being shot for fur.

"No emotion," Kuyasaki said. "Not now. Emotion makes you loud."

Myasako became calm again.

Kuyasaki walked across the room of rugs and wooden floorboards, and approached a large, circular metal door. There was a keypad on the wall.

Kuyasaki typed in the combination he had heard the assistant say. The metal door popped open, and from behind them down the stairs they could hear sudden angry words and shouting.

"Asleep! Why are you asleep?! You know you should always be awake!"

They heard the assistant begin to run up the stairs.

"Come!" the assistant barked at the girl. "You are to stand outside the vault door now, as a last resort. Others will take your place at the bottom of the stairs."

Kuyasaki pulled open the large metal vault door, and beckoned the other two inside. The three ninjas ran in, and pulled the door shut behind them. It creaked. Loudly.

"What was that?" they heard the assistant ask. "That was the vault door!"

Kuyasaki bolted the door shut from the inside.

"Come!" Kuyasaki said, beginning to run through the narrow stone corridor they were now in. They turned a corner, and there was a huge gap in the floor. There was a chasm between them and the little dark doorway standing across from them.

It was too dark to see where the gap in the floor led down to.

"Can you make it?" Kuyasaki asked Myasako.

"Yes."

Myasako watched his father leap across the gap and land silently on the other side, crouching low as he landed.

"It's far," Kuyasaki said. "Use Takashi as a spring."

They had practiced this before. Takashi crouched down and offered his hands, palms up.

Myasako stood on Takashi's palms, and as Takashi exploded upwards into a vertical leap, Myasako sprang himself off and flew through the air. He landed on the other side.

They heard banging on the vault door from around the corner. Then they heard alarms going off.

Takashi took a few steps back, and launched himself across the gap in the ground. On the other side, they saw there was a plank of wood that had been kicked away.

They began running into near darkness, and then stopped.

Kuyasaki looked up, and above them was a final little doorway, high up inside the stone wall.

There was nothing leading up to it, but the walls were jagged and rough.

"Wait for us at the top, Myasako," Kuyasaki said.

Takashi and Kuyasaki kneeled to give Myasako a boost. They launched him so high that he nearly reached the little doorway at once. He grabbed on to the protruding rocks of the wall, and looked down to see his father and Takashi climbing up the wall like spiders. Myasako entered the little doorway, and standing in front of him, sitting in candlelight, eating a chicken, was his uncle Senzi.

Senzi hadn't noticed him yet. Kuyasaki walked in behind Myasako, overtook him, and sprinted towards Senzi.

Senzi looked up at the last moment, grabbed at his gun, but Kuyasaki disarmed him and pinned him to the ground.

"Why have you been doing this?" Kuyasaki said. He sounded fiery. He was hissing in his brother's face. "Why?"

He was nearly choking Senzi, who was beginning to wheeze.

"You know I just wanted some of your money," Senzi said.

"I think you wanted more. I think you wanted Myasako to work for you, to be of use to you as you expand your operations."

"What operations?" Senzi still had chicken in his mouth.

"I know you are building and selling weapons, deep underground. I know that's how you can sustain a compound like this, and you want to expand, with as many warriors to protect you as possible."

Senzi tried to change the subject.

"How did you even get in here? Didn't my daughter try to stop you?"

"She was deeply asleep. You clearly ask too much of her."

"Asleep! Again! I'm training her to not need sleep."

"I'm here, Dad!" They all heard a young female's voice come from above, and on top of Kuyasaki landed the sleeping ninja from the stairway, now fiercely awake, beginning to choke Kuyasaki with her legs while striking him on the head. Myasako leapt up and went to choke her, but she sensed him leaping, she ducked, and continued strangling Kuyasaki.

Kuyasaki knew it was his niece, his niece who he had never met, but he was starting to lose consciousness. The world was becoming even darker.

Takashi drew his sword, but had been told by Kuyasaki to not kill any children. Otherwise, Takashi would have done it already, and killed Senzi at the same time.

Senzi went to grab his gun. Myasako kicked it away and struck him on the side of the head with another kick. Senzi went limp.

"My father!" the girl yelled, launching herself at Myasako. Myasako had no ideas of her being related to him, and his instinct made him punch her straight in the mouth. She stumbled back into Takashi's arms, who held her still for a moment, trying to suppress his instinct to snap her neck, until she stamped on his foot and threw him over her back and went at Myasako again.

She was incredibly fast and nimble, and Myasako felt himself being hit again and again. He grabbed hold of her, and he felt her reach for her daggers.

Myasako trapped her arms, kicked her at the knee so that she fell down, and he knelt on top of her. She rolled him off, then she knelt on top of him and pulled out a dagger from behind her.

She thrust the dagger towards Myasako's throat, but he slid out of the way, just, he trapped her arm again and moved his hips away to the side of her. He kicked her away, stood, and took out his nunchuks.

With nunchuks, Myasako was deadly. He went towards the girl, and caught her on the arm, making her drop her dagger. She took out a small metal cylinder with her other hand, threw it on the ground, and the whole room turned to smoke. Myasako couldn't see. He could hear his father spluttering and coughing, and Myasako was crouched down low, ready to defend against any strikes.

The smoke lingered, settled, and as it cleared, the girl and her father were gone.

消滅する

Vanish

Chapter 8 - The Overwhelm

As time passed, no danger approached Martin, his mother or Nerris. No authorities had returned to the house. Martin's stone hadn't moved. Everything seemed normal. Still, Nerris would often stay up all night, waiting by the door, looking out the window onto the road, holding the Demonstraliser in her arms. Then she would sleep for a few hours late in the morning.

"Are you okay?" Martin's mother asked her. "You're barely sleeping."

"Oh, I don't sleep much anyway," Nerris said, yawning as she came downstairs for lunch. "I'm fine, I'm fine, thank you."

Martin was already eating. His face was in his plate and he was licking his bowl. Nerris had been trying to convince his mother that it was safe to reset his DNA to normal using one of her machines in the basement.

"Martin?" Nerris said. Martin looked up and grunted.

"We really need to do something about your behaviour now. I know you can't feel it, but you're gradually losing who you are. You're turning into a tiger on the inside."

Martin yawned and didn't pay her much attention. He wanted to go and lie in the sun now that he had eaten.

"Yes, I agree," his mother said, seeing that she was gradually losing her son more and more by the day. "Martin, we need to get you fixed. Can't you get the stone to turn you back to normal? You have been barely speaking recently, and sometimes I hear you snarling in the night. I'm worried."

Martin looked at the two of them with piercing eyes.

"I'm fine," he said. "I've told you before, I'm fine. I feel stronger than ever. I'm going out."

"Where?" his mother said. He knew he wasn't allowed out by himself at the moment.

"I'm just going for a walk. By myself. Alone. I need to get out of this house. I want to look for small things that I can catch."

"No," his mother said, getting up and standing in front of the door.

"Let me out, Mum. I mean it. Let me out."

"No."

Martin's mother didn't move, and Martin crouched down low and let out a tremendous roar, a roar so loud that it shook his mother's bones, and Nerris quickly disappeared downstairs into the basement.

"Nerris!" Martin's mother called.

Martin turned around and began to run towards the back door. He unlocked it, stepped out, and in one leap, he cleared the garden fence and disappeared.

Nerris came running back up the stairs.

"Come on, let's go," she said to her sister, following after Martin and holding a small tranquiliser gun. "He's going hunting."

*

Nerris was trundling along the pavement, watching Martin in the distance. She was holding her dart gun under her poncho. Martin's mother was struggling to keep up.

"Will that hurt him?" she said to Nerris.

"No. Well...yes, it will hurt a lot for about a second, then it will send him to sleep. We need to get him back home before he harms someone."

Martin was far ahead down the street, and he stopped and looked behind him. He saw Nerris and his mother chasing him down, and he took off towards the woods in the distance. He was running tremendously fast.

"We'll never catch him," Martin's mother said. "Look how fast he's running!"

"We can catch him," Nerris said. She pulled out her ancient-looking mobile phone and found a number. She dialled.

"Horridge? Horridge it's Nerris. No, no I don't want to talk about that now, I need a favour. There is a young boy about to run past your house. I need you to tranquilise him. He's my nephew, he's becoming dangerous. Brown hair. Blue trousers that look a bit too small. I can't explain why, just trust me, please. Once you've done it we'll need to borrow your wheelbarrow. Okay. Okay, thanks. We'll be there soon.

"Come on, hurry up," Nerris said. "Horridge is a really good shot."

*

Nerris and her sister arrived to find Martin lying on the floor by the woods. His body had grown considerably over the last few days. He was still slightly conscious. There was a large green wheelbarrow beside him.

"Martin! Martin!" his mother gasped. "Is he okay?"

"He's fine. Horridge has a brilliant tranquiliser blend. It's non-toxic, but he won't share the recipe with anyone else. He says he's waiting to sell it to the military at the right time. Anyway, let's get Martin in this wheelbarrow and get him back home."

"Mum, Mum I want to go and catch something," Martin muttered as Nerris hoisted his body into the wheelbarrow.

"Okay, okay, dear," Martin's mother said. "Okay, we're on our way."

*

When they got home, they carried Martin into the basement. Martin was waking up.

"Why am I back here? I want to go hunting!" Martin said. His voice was regaining its strength, and he was starting to struggle. His voice was deeper than normal.

"Put him on here," Nerris said, holding Martin by the feet and placing them on a wooden workbench. Martin's mother helped move the rest of him.

"Now strap in his wrists."

Nerris strapped down Martin's feet so he couldn't move.

"Don't we need masks down here?" Martin's mother said.

"Not anymore," Nerris said.

Martin's mother strapped down his wrists, reluctantly.

"You're sure this is safe?" she asked.

"Um...yeh. Like I've said, it's never been tested on a human before, but...I can't see why it wouldn't work.

"It's supposed to purify his DNA to match the majority of his system," Nerris continued. "He's still more human than tiger, but we have to act soon."

Nerris pulled out a large syringe that was attached to an extendable metal arm, clamped onto the edge of her workbench. She adjusted it to hover over Martin's stomach.

"Put these on," Nerris said, handing Martin's mother some dark glasses.

Nerris put some on herself, and put some over Martin's eyes.

"Nerris, I'm not sure about this," Martin's mother said.

"He's never going to ask for the stone or anyone else to fix him," Nerris said. "The tiger inside him is not a conscious thing. It is unconscious, taking over everything about him. He'll be able to fight well, but soon he might actually start turning orange, growing fur, claws, all the rest."

"Well maybe that's okay, I just don't know what this contraption of yours could do. Once you turned that frog into a horse, and..."

"Oh, but that was ages ago! And I fixed it, eventually. That frog ended up with more endurance than any other of his kind. He could hop for miles. He was better off."

Nerris looked down. "Look at Martin's arms," she said.

They looked at Martin's arms. The arms looked far more hairy than normal. Slightly orange.

"Come on. You know that even if I mess things up, I always fix them in the end. Come on. Give me the word," Nerris said.

Martin's mother was contracted into herself, holding her hands on her chin.

"Oh, just do it then! Quick!"

Nerris flicked a switch on the side of the syringe, pressed a button, and the whole room was filled with light.

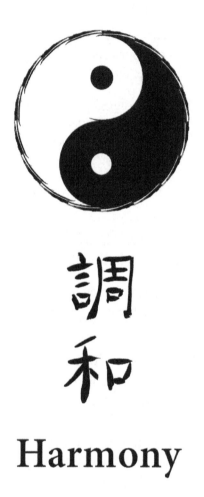

調
和

Harmony

Chapter 9 - Ascension

"Where did they go?" Myasako said, looking around for Senzi and the young girl.

Takashi pointed upwards.

They all looked up, and there was another small doorway, even higher above them than the one before.

Now they heard guards approaching.

"Where's the plank? Where's the plank?" they heard an angry voice shouting. The guards were at the chasm from before, unable to cross.

"We have to escape here, now, or we fight them once they find their way across," Kuyasaki said.

"Let's fight," Myasako said. He wondered how the girl could have carried Senzi so high up the wall by herself, so quietly.

"Your emotion is speaking for you," Kuyasaki said. "I let myself become distracted when facing my brother. I failed you both, I should have heard her coming."

"So who is she?"

"She is Nayla. She is Senzi's daughter. Takashi, let's go."

Takashi took out what looked like a small gun from his pocket. He aimed and fired it at the door high above them. Out shot a cable which stuck to the wall just above the doorway.

"Grab hold of Takashi," Kuyasaki said.

They both grabbed hold of Takashi's body, and whilst he held the cable gun, they were carried high up the wall towards the door.

"I thought these were too noisy to use?" Myasako said.

"But we must use them when we have no other choice."

"Where does this doorway lead?"

Kuyasaki looked down as the guards began to flood into the room, too loud with their thoughts and footsteps and emotions to notice the three ninjas escaping above them.

"Where this door leads, I do not know," Kuyasaki said.

The three infiltrating ninjas ascended, being taken up towards the archway high up in the wall.

"There they are!" they heard a guard call from below.

Gunshots were fired, just as Myasako, Kuyasaki and Takashi made it into the darkness and temporary safety of the archway.

Myasako looked out, and there were bursts of pink and red flying up into the wall.

"What are they?" Myasako asked.

"They are from Senzi's weapons. He is building his own, beginning to sell them to mobs all over the world. He also kidnaps children."

"What? Why?"

"He is building an army, an army of evil ninjas that will serve Senzi to the death. His daughter is his best student. She will surely die for him, and he has trained her since birth, as I did you."

The three ninjas began to move along a dark, cave-like passageway.

"So she is my cousin?" Myasako said.

"It's best not to think of her like that, not while she is ready to kill you."

The three ninjas climbed down a ledge, and below them was a pool of dark water. Deep beneath the water there was a very small yellow light.

"Down there. We have to swim down."

"How do you know?" Myasako said.

"I don't know how. I just feel it," Kuyasaki said. "When you are silent enough inside, connected enough to your surroundings, solutions begin to yield themselves. But you have to trust them. I will go first."

Kuyasaki jumped, and dove straight into the water. Takashi and Myasako watched as he swam down, and then swam back up to the surface.

"Come!" he whispered up towards the two as his head appeared above the water. "Come! Quick!"

Myasako jumped, landing in the water and beginning to kick and swim downwards. He could see a light in the distance beneath him, and heard a plunging noise as Takashi dove into the water behind him.

Myasako watched as Kuyasaki swam towards the light, where there was an air pocket just beyond it. Kuyasaki's legs disappeared up into it.

Myasako followed, swam just beneath the light, and emerged upwards into a huge tunnel, big enough for a train to fit through.

As he climbed out of the water, Takashi emerged behind them.

"Can you sense that?" Kuyasaki said.

Myasako nodded. They were being watched from somewhere. Something had eyes on them.

The three ninjas looked around, and began to move forward along the tunnel. They could sense a slight pressure pushing down on their skin, as if something was about to happen.

And then from a large crevice in the wall up ahead, out jumped Senzi and his daughter, Nayla.

Senzi was wielding a huge grey rifle that he had to hold with two hands, and as he went to fire on them, Takashi took out a throwing dart, and threw it straight into Senzi's throat.

Senzi let off a shot with his rifle that burst out a shooting red beam at the ceiling. It made the inside of the tunnel crumble slightly, and Senzi fell back, clutching at his neck.

"Father!" Nayla shouted. "Attack them!"

Suddenly Nayla began to charge, filled with rage, and twenty other young ninjas appeared out of the darkness in the distance, all holding swords and daggers and nunchuks and throwing darts.

Some were older than Myasako – teenagers, bigger, bulkier and heavier. Others were close to his age – lighter and more nimble. He could see the way they were wielding their weapons that they had been training for a while.

Nayla began to throw darts at Takashi, who could shift his body and catch them as she threw them.

Takashi then drew his sword.

"Don't kill any of them!" Kuyasaki yelled, as Nayla approached them with twenty ninja kids behind her, and a battle ensued.

Kuyasaki, Takashi and Myasako had to fight off and disable all of Senzi's young soldiers without killing any of them. Takashi would touch them on their necks, and the kids would drop as if they would go to sleep. Myasako hadn't developed this touch yet, and was kicking the soldiers in the stomachs as they attacked him. Kuyasaki began to wave his hands in the air, and the armed children and teens were being knocked back and sticking to the walls.

But Nayla was harder to control.

She would be brushed away by Kuyasaki's ninja wave, but she would bounce back off the walls and attack again. She would swing her sword, slicing at anything she could, and Kuyasaki sometimes had to duck and slide and move his body before he brushed her away again without touching her.

Takashi was still surrounded by a group of young aggressors armed with daggers and little knives, and as he moved away from strikes and stabs, he would touch pressure points on their necks to drop more of them to the ground.

Myasako caught Nayla with her back to him, and he grabbed her arms to trap them and he took her to the ground away from the others.

He held her there while he watched other young assassins drop to sleep or stick to the walls, but soon Nayla was free again, now on top of him, ready to dig her sword into his chest.

As she did, Myasako guided the smooth side of the sword away from his body, reached up, wrapped his arms around her neck and began to squeeze. He was squeezing his fist into a major artery in her neck.

She started digging her fingers into his eyes, but he could feel her drifting off slowly, squirming but drifting off into sleep.

Then she went limp. He let go, but she was tricking him. She sat up and they started to fight again.

It wasn't until they all heard another rifle shot, that everything stopped.

Senzi was standing, still with a dart in his throat, holding his rifle again.

"Come here, Nayla," he said with a weak and raspy voice, pointing his weapon at Takashi, Myasako and Kuyasaki.

This time Takashi threw another dart, but Nayla struck it away with her sword.

"Release my ninjas, and come with me," Senzi said to the three intruders.

"Okay," Kuyasaki said to Senzi. "We have been caught."

Out of the corner of his eye, Myasako saw Kuyasaki reaching for his own throwing darts. Then from behind them came spluttering, gasping noises as armed guards with more rifles appeared, having just swam down as the three ninjas had before.

"There they are," one of the spluttering guards yelled, running towards them, pointing his weapon at the three of them.

"Myasako. Jump on my back right now."

Myasako heard the voice of his father directly in his head. He had never heard it quite so clearly.

"Do it!" he heard his father scream within him. Myasako jumped on his father's back, and Kuyasaki and Takashi ran off silently to the wall on the side of the large tunnel.

"What the...where did they go?" the guard said, now joined by five others, dripping wet and looking exhausted.

"I don't believe it," Senzi said. "They've mastered invisibility! How?! Why not before! They must be here. Fire! Start firing!"

The guards hesitated.

"Fire, just fire anywhere!" Senzi yelled, grabbing his daughter and dragging her off to the crevice where they were hiding before.

Myasako clung on to his father's back like a little ape as Kuyasaki and Takashi sprinted off away down the tunnel, staying close to the wall as shots fired past them. Kuyasaki rolled, and Myasako felt a blazing heat skim over the top of his head. They kept running, and the shots became scarcer.

"Where are they?! We were so close to having them all!" Senzi yelled, and the three ninjas were gone.

超
能
力

Supernatural
Power

Chapter 10 - Freedom

"Mum? Nerris? What's happening? Why am I strapped down?"

Martin's body had returned to normal. It was normal size, normal shape, and without a layer of fur beginning to form on the arms.

"Oh, thank goodness," Martin's mother said, wrapping her arms around him. "Thank goodness. Unstrap him, Nerris."

"Wait," Nerris said. "Martin. I have some meat upstairs. It's not cooked at the moment. Shall I bring it down for you?"

Martin furrowed his eyebrows and looked at Nerris.

"Wh...why? You mean raw? I don't know about that, Nerris..."

"Okay, we can unstrap him," Nerris said. "Do you feel normal, Martin?"

"Yes. I feel lighter than before. But I can't remember how I got here."

"That's okay. Do you still have your stone?"

"Yes, it's in my pocket."

"Okay. Okay then," Nerris said.

*

As the days went by, things were still quiet for Martin, his mother and Nerris. His mother was becoming more and more uneasy as each day passed without being chased down or investigated by any people under Jacobson's influence.

She was becoming paranoid, and would spend a lot of her time staring out of the window from the living room.

Nerris was talking to Martin at the dinner table about life, repeatedly emphasising to him the importance of persistence in order to achieve great things.

"Never stop! Never stop!" she was saying. "If there's something you want to do, never stop!"

Martin was listening, chewing his food quietly.

He felt like his old self again, but couldn't help but miss some of the power he felt inside him when his inner tiger began to take him over.

"I still want to learn more about how to fight," he said to Nerris at the table. "When I was in Japan I learnt some things, but not enough. I don't want to have to rely on a magic stone my whole life. I want to learn more."

"Well I can help you with that," Nerris said.

"How?" Martin said. His mother was standing at the window, looking out of the curtains for any sign of marauders.

"Well," Nerris said. "I've picked it up over the years. I've been in a few scraps, and lived with some people who were born warriors. People all over the world – here in England, overseas in cities, in jungles – all over the place. If you want to learn more about how to fight, I can teach you. With your mother's permission of course.

"Amanda?" Nerris asked. "Is it alright if I start to teach Martin some more fighting tricks?"

"Yes...fine," Martin's mother said. She was distant, far away from them in her mind.

"And maybe you could join in too," Nerris said. "You gotta stop living in fear, Amanda. It's taking you over. A constant state of fear only attracts more of itself. You're doing yourself no good. You've seen what Martin's stone can do. I've got the Demonstraliser always at the ready. We'll be okay."

Amanda looked at Nerris.

"Okay. You're right," she said, trying to shake the fear off her, and walking back to the table. "Okay, let's all do some training then, Nerris. Where shall we go? In the garden? In here?"

"Actually, I've got another idea," Nerris said. "Let's go to the woods."

*

After what felt like hours of climbing, traversing, creeping and running, the three Japanese ninjas were on top of Senzi's compound, standing on the roof, overlooking the high iron fences surrounding them and the forest in the distance.

"This place is huge," Myasako said. "How can he afford all of this?"

"The weapons industry is extremely profitable," Kuyasaki said. "Senzi makes his money in other ways too, ways that I dare not utter to you."

"You never told me you had mastered invisibility," Myasako said. "Why have you never taught me about that?"

"Because it's best when powers like that begin to manifest themselves of their own accord," Kuyasaki said. "For invisibility to manifest at the right moments, you have to be completely free from yourself. It must be as if you don't exist as a separate entity – you are just a piece of life flowing, dancing, and life cloaks you with invisibility when the time is right. I still don't feel as if I have complete mastery over it. It seems to happen without me trying to summon it. I cannot teach what is so mysterious, but I teach you what has led me to this point."

"Well what now?" Myasako said. "Those children, they were so loyal to him. Why?"

"Brainwashing. He wipes their memories and replaces them with his own ideas. They all believe he is their father, so they naturally want to do anything to protect him."

"Can we free them?"

"Yes. But I'm not sure how yet."

"What do we do? Do we leave or go back for more?"

"Again, I am not sure. When the answers are not clear, we must become silent. We must focus on a solution, be in tune with any possible solutions or next steps that will lead us to the highest good for all. Takashi will keep guard. Sit with me, let a solution form itself inside of us."

Kuyasaki and Myasako both sat on the roof of Senzi's criminal compound, shut their eyes, and began to meditate, to create space in themselves for the next step to take.

瞑
想

Meditation

Chapter 11 - Meeting Aggression

"Sir, they've gone into the forest."

Jacobson Muldridge was standing in his underground viewing room again, with the same three technicians manning the remote cameras and videos. They could see Martin, his mother and Nerris walking through the little town, towards the forest, and disappearing into it. Nerris was carrying a huge bag with one arm.

"The forest? Are they mad? No one ever goes into the forest anymore. Haven't they heard about what might be out there?" Jacobson said.

"I don't know, sir. All the microphones we dropped in the area don't seem to be working. All we can hear is static, as if they have been sabotaged..."

"Now's our chance," Jacobson said. "If we can get to them in the forest – I'll bet they've got the protective stone on them. That's all I want. Just get me that. Don't seek to harm them. When we had those fake police officers go to their home, the stone didn't activate because they weren't seeking to harm anyone. We will do the same. That might keep the stone dormant."

"Shall I send out a team, sir? We can't see them under the cover of trees, but we can get a team to drop into the woods and do a search. Some are already close by."

"Yes. And I'm going. I don't want anyone touching that stone except for me. What do you think was in that huge bag of hers?"

"Not sure, sir."

"Get a team ready. A large team. I'm going too."

*

While sitting on the roof of Senzi's compound, Kuyasaki and Myasako both had a flashing vision of guards racing up a stairwell behind them. There were many guards, many armed guards with the same young ninjas from before crawling up the walls on every side of the building. They were becoming surrounded. Uncle Senzi was somewhere behind the guards, keeping his distance.

They heard Takashi draw his sword. Myasako and Kuyasaki stood to their feet.

"We have to end this," Kuyasaki said. "If we flee now, he will chase us down again and again. I have showed his men enough mercy. Now we must do whatever our instincts tell us. There are no more rules over who to destroy and who to spare. If someone is threatening your life, do what you must to protect yourself. Is that understood?"

"Understood," Myasako said, and as a swarm of guards piled in through a doorway to the roof in the distance, Takashi held his sword high beside him and began to sprint toward the guards, to do what he had been wanting to do since he arrived.

The guards were no issue for Takashi. As more piled in through the door onto the roof, more would fall to the ground. Myasako watched, and was surprised at how compassionate Takashi was. Myasako expected blood and slicing, but in Takashi's freedom, not much blood was shed. The men looked more like they were falling down to nap.

Then Senzi's young ninjas appeared at all four sides after climbing the walls. They charged again.

"Hold this," Kuyasaki said, handing Myasako his sword. Myasako took the sword, and Kuyasaki grabbed him by the feet, and began to swing him around in a circle. He swung him around so fast it created a slicing barrier between them and the surrounding ninjas. They all stopped, hesitant, not wanting to be cut. And then Nayla appeared, jumping off the shoulders of a tall young ninja holding a sword himself, and she descended down towards the head of Kuyasaki. Kuyasaki let his son go, and Myasako went spinning into some of the assassins surrounding him, making them duck and move out of the way.

Now Myasako stood near the edge of the building, and he began to fight. He fought with everything he had, surrounded by young assailants, kicking, punching, grabbing, throwing, biting, gouging, stomping and kneeing his way through anyone who came close to him with aggression. He became so charged with ferociousness, channelled ferociousness, that many of the young ninjas began to back away. He was like a blur, a blurring whirlwind of fury that knocked back or knocked unconscious anything it touched. Soon Takashi was with him to help, and he was throwing these assailants over the side of the compound. They would land on the ground, roll, and begin to flee.

The only one still fighting was Nayla.

Kuyasaki had her pinned to the ground. She was struggling but he was too heavy and had all of her limbs trapped under his.

He was saying something to her, but Myasako couldn't make out what he was saying.

She was screaming "No! No I will always fight for my father!"

Takashi drew his sword again. There was a true coldness that emanated from him for a moment, and for the first time, Myasako saw him as he truly was – an assassin that would do anything to keep those closest to him safe. He had been saved by

Kuyasaki at a young age, trained by him, and felt as if he owed Kuyasaki his life. Now he was ready to do anything.

As Kuyasaki held Nayla down, she was struggling herself into exhaustion.

Myasako looked up, and saw Senzi at the doorway to the rooftop, looking from behind the arch.

He stepped out of the archway, holding his rifle, now with bandages wrapped around his throat.

"Let her go, Kuyasaki."

Takashi threw a ninja star at Senzi's hand, making him drop his weapon. He and Myasako both charged, throwing more ninja stars at the man, preventing him from picking up the rifle. Senzi retreated back out of the door, and Takashi picked up his weapon.

They both ran back to Kuyasaki.

"Look," Kuyasaki said to Nayla. "He only sees you as a soldier. Did he ever tell you what happened to your mother?"

Nayla looked at Kuyasaki. For the first time, he had her full attention on what he was saying.

"He told me. He told me she left us."

"We are leaving now," Kuyasaki said. "You must ask him to take you to the fifth basement, and see who is in there. If he doesn't show you, it's because your mother is being kept there, behind bars. You must speak with her. She is a force of good. He has some kind of powerful dark spell over the area, something that I cannot penetrate with my mind, or with my body. He has something in this compound that can produce dark powerful spells, and I don't know where that is, either. I can only sense its presence. Demand to see the fifth basement, or else you will never know the truth. After all...what's the harm in seeing a basement?"

Another wave of guards appeared at the door. Kuyasaki grabbed hold of Myasako, and he nodded to Takashi. The guards watched as these three crouching ninjas disappeared into the space around them, and left the compound for good.

*

Myasako had the same feeling as when he had first jumped into the pool of water to be transported, except now it was easier. Connected to his father, his father was carrying him along a teleportation tunnel that was flashing with blues and greens. Soon the three ninjas appeared back in the mountainside, standing in the cave, looking down on the pool of water from before.

"As your skills develop, you will also be able to travel through the ether, at will, to anywhere you need to be," Kuyasaki said to his son. "But in the absence of open air, it is extremely difficult. That is why Senzi's compound has so few windows – it stifles some of the powers that could be used against him."

"What do you think Nayla will do?" Myasako said.

"She will ask him to see the fifth basement. She will not stop asking until she finds out what's in there. She is highly intelligent, cunning and determined. It is only through her conditioning that she seeks to support her father's intentions. If she sees him for what he really is, she will become independent, a truly powerful human being in her own right, a servant to no ill-minded master."

There was a pause. Takashi was staring into the pool of water, and so was Myasako.

"Will they ever come back for us – for me?" Myasako said.

"I don't know. There is a dark energy holding his plans together, ruling over his compound. As long as that darkness persists, Senzi is still dangerous."

"What about calling the police?" Myasako said. "What about the kids he has trapped in there?"

"The authorities know that invading Senzi's compound could trigger a civil war, gangs versus police, where many more innocent people would be hurt. There is a great fear of confronting Senzi where he lives. We have to trust that Nayla will begin to dismantle the operation from the inside once she realises the truth."

The three ninjas began to walk out of the cave in the side of the mountain, and Kuyasaki spoke again.

"Now, as we are here, do you want to do any more training, or have you had enough for one day?"

Myasako looked at Takashi, who smiled a slight smile.

"Let's go home," Myasako said.

家
庭

Home

Chapter 12 - The Garganfan

Martin, his mother and Nerris were walking through the woods. It was extremely quiet.

"Nerris, I don't like this," Martin's mother said. "Everyone knows you should keep away from the woods. It's too quiet in here."

"Oh, nonsense," Nerris said, carrying something in a huge bag by her side. "People don't know anything."

"Why have we come out here?"

"There's someone out here who can help teach Martin how to fight. Well, not someone...some *thing.*"

Martin's mother stopped.

"No. No I don't like it. We've all heard the stories and we all know they're not true. But still I don't like it, I feel like something is watching us."

All three of them stopped. The rustling of the leaves beneath their feet stopped, and it was perfectly quiet.

"Not far to go now," Nerris said "You don't have to stay, Amanda. Do you want to keep going, Martin?"

Martin nodded.

"Don't worry, Mum, Nerris has brought her Demonstraliser anyway, we'll be fine. Won't we, Nerris? Your Demonstraliser can stop anything that tries to harm us. Plus I've got my stone. We'll be fine."

Martin's mother reluctantly followed as Nerris walked on ahead. Nerris had never told them that she hadn't tested it on humans before. Only dogs.

"Here we are," Nerris said. "He lives up here somewhere. Apparently there are more of his kind spread far throughout the forest, but I've only ever seen one."

"Seen what?" Martin said.

"A Garganfan," Nerris said.

Nerris began to call up into the trees.

"Garganfan? Where are you?"

And then they heard a cracking from above. Branches sounded like they were cracking and breaking from the huge trees overhead, and one large branch began to fall swiftly to the ground. As it flew down towards them, Martin saw it begin to morph and form the shape of a man – a long, thin, branch-like man with an oddly cone-shaped head.

The Garganfan crouched low as it landed, and they all felt the ground shake a little bit.

It looked up at Nerris as it stood. It had beady dark eyes.

"You asked for it, Nerris," it said.

Suddenly the Garganfan charged at Nerris and swung a punch at her face. Nerris ducked under the punch, reached up from behind the Garganfan and began to cling to its neck. Then she started to squeeze.

"Not my neck!" the Garganfan wheezed, and then it couldn't speak. Nerris was choking it. The Garganfan collapsed to its knees and tried to throw Nerris over his shoulder, but Nerris hooked her heels in between the front of the Garganfan's legs, so that she was clinging on to him like a young ape on its mother's back. Then the Garganfan collapsed onto the floor, and stopped moving.

Nerris stood up, and brushed herself off.

"Ah," she said brightly. "Well, this is the Garganfan."

The Garganfan began to stir, and got back up to its knees.

"Did I go out just then?" the Garganfan said. "Damn!" The Garganfan started hammering the ground with its fists. It hated to lose any fight.

Martin's mother felt like she couldn't breathe as she watched.

"I've told you, you give up your back far too easily," Nerris said. "Now, meet my nephew, Martin, and my sister, Amanda."

"Nice to meet you," the Garganfan said, standing to attention and not moving.

"Now it's your turn, Martin," Nerris said.

"No way," Martin's mother said. "No, he's not fighting that thing."

"Don't worry!" Nerris said. "This one doesn't go overboard. He matches your skill, but is slightly better in places to make sure you improve. He won't overwhelm Martin."

"It's still dangerous. Come on, Martin. Let's go."

Martin's mother grabbed him by the arm, and began to drag him away.

"But I want to learn from the Garganfan!"

"That's not learning, that's just fighting," his mother said.

And then all four of them heard a very soft, very low drumming, chopping sound. It was coming from somewhere above the trees. It sounded like a helicopter, a quiet helicopter that didn't want to be noticed, just above the forest so the occupants could peer down into the woods.

"Oh no. That's them," Nerris said. She reached for her bag and took out the Demonstraliser. She pushed a button on the side for it to begin waking up. A green light appeared and began to shine brightly toward the Garganfan, who squinted and shielded his dark eyes.

"Get behind me," Nerris said. "Everyone."

"Who's coming?" the Garganfan said.

"Bad people," Nerris said. "Very bad people. They've come to take something from Martin."

"Well, I'm up for a fight," the Garganfan said, limbering up. "You've never seen me when I'm not training someone, Nerris. You've never seen what I can do."

The hovering got louder, and from directly above them, a small group of men dressed in black began to descend down a cable, to land in front of them all.

The last one to be carried down was Jacobson Muldridge. He was holding on to the back of his largest guard, strapped to the guard's back with cables and locks.

Nerris aimed her Demonstraliser at him as he landed.

"Unstrap me!" Jacobson called as he landed on the ground, and the helicopter above began to rise up and reduce the noise. The team crowded around Jacobson, unstrapped him, and he was standing there, in a suit.

The hovering sound disappeared.

"I'll shoot, and you'll never be the same," Nerris said, pointing the Demonstraliser at him. She still wasn't sure if it might accidentally kill someone.

"Just give me the word, Nerris," the Garganfan said.

"Not yet," Nerris whispered.

"We mean no harm, we come in peace," Jacobson said, raising his arms and taking a little step forward.

"All we have come for is the stone that Martin possesses, that is all. And I do not want to steal it. I want to buy it from you. I will pay you twenty million pounds for the stone, Martin, for you to hand it over to me willingly. I can transfer the money to your account right now."

Jacobson took out his phone and showed the amount on his screen. Martin could hardly see, he was a bit too far away.

"So what do you say?" Jacobson smiled. "The stone, in return for a life of luxury, ease, and no more hassle from me?"

Martin looked at his mother. He could do so much for her with that money. He could buy her anything she wanted, take her anywhere she'd like to go...

Then he thought of Kuyasaki, who was standing in front of him, shaking his head left and right furiously. Martin thought of what Jacobson would do in the world, to people, to countries, if he knew he couldn't be touched, if he had dragons or even bigger creatures that might emerge out of the stone to protect him.

"No," Martin said.

The stone in his pocket started to tremble.

"No?" Jacobson said. His face started to twitch slightly. He remembered to not have any violent thoughts towards Martin, and to just focus on the stone.

He just wanted that stone.

"Well," Jacobson said, taking another step forward. "What if I've found a way around your little stone's mentality? What if it only wakes up when *you* are threatened, as the owner? What if it doesn't respond to people being threatened around you?"

Jacobson clicked his fingers, and one of his guards pulled out a large wooden gun from behind his waist. He pointed it at Martin's mother, fired, and a heavy net shot out and sailed through the air and landed on top of Martin's mother, knocking her back and making her hit her head on the trunk of a tree. She went limp, and Martin went rushing over.

"Now!" Nerris yelled to the Garganfan, and she blasted all four guards with an enormous beam of green light that exploded from her Demonstraliser, catching Jacobson as she did so.

The Garganfan jumped into the beam, and began knocking down and disarming all the men at the same time.

Martin was knelt beside his mother, trying to wake her up and untangle her body from the net. He briefly turned around to see the Garganfan jumping between men, viciously making them pay for what one of them had just done.

Nerris was struggling to control the power of the beam that was blasting on all the men, and suddenly the beam died away.

"It needs to recharged," she said, putting it on the ground. "It charges faster if it touches the earth..."

Then they heard more noise. More men were approaching them in the distance, walking quickly along the forest floor holding more nets and weapons that Nerris could not quite make out.

"Run!" Nerris said, picking up her Demonstraliser which was only half-charged. She ran over to Martin, picked her sister up from the ground in one hoist, and began to sprint in the other direction of the men.

"Come on Martin!" she yelled.

Martin started sprinting too, struggling to catch up with Nerris who looked like she was a soldier in the military, running quickly at a chugging, consistent pace.

Then Nerris started to slow down again. Martin could hear men yelling and screaming from behind him as the Garganfan started to attack them as they approached, but as Nerris slowed down, Martin did too.

There were more men in the distance, all dressed in black, all walking through the trees and approaching very slowly, more of them holding nets and sticks and all sorts of weapons that wouldn't make any noise in the forest to attract attention.

Martin's mother started to stir. The back of her head was bleeding. She was still covered in a thick net.

"What's happening?" she said, looking around, confused.

Nerris put her sister down.

"The Demonstraliser still isn't charged!" Nerris hissed to Martin, putting it on the ground to try to make it charge faster.

"What are we going to do?" Martin said to Nerris, and Nerris rolled up her sleeves.

"We're going to have to fight," Nerris said. "Just think, Martin, if any one of them tries to harm you, any one of them, your stone will wake up. It protects the owner. You'll be indestructible."

"Well..." Martin hesitated. He didn't think he could fight off all the men, even if they didn't try to harm him. He didn't want to leave his mother's side.

"What if I just give the stone to Mum? If I give the stone to her, it will protect her – the stone will wake up and protect her. They aren't going for me, they are going after *her*."

Martin took the stone from his pocket and placed it in his mother's hands.

"Here you go, Mum, take this."

His mother was losing consciousness again. The men were getting gradually closer.

"Mum!"

"It's not working, Martin," Nerris said. "She can't accept it the way she is. But even if she did – then what? Then they might come back and come after you. Or me. We'll always be running. We need to end this. Come on. I'll go first."

Nerris stood and faced the oncoming men. Martin felt a burning anger begin to rise inside of him. They had hurt his mother.

"I can't see a real gun anywhere," Nerris said quietly. "They don't want to attract too much attention to themselves..."

At that moment they heard quick, flaring footsteps approaching them from behind, and the Garganfan leapt over Martin and Nerris, and started charging at the men ahead of them.

"Aaaggghhh!" The Garganfan let out a huge battle cry which seemed to shake the trees, and Martin was so overcome by the sound, he stood up, and he began charging at the men.

"Aaaggghhh!" Martin shouted as well, and as he charged directly at one of the men, the stone in his pocket started to shake. The men couldn't help but think of harming Martin in some way, at least grabbing him and holding him down to shut him up, or even worse – ending this whole thing so they could go home and stop worrying about protective stones, and as Martin got closer and closer, with Nerris sprinting beside him, the stone exploded out of his pocket, and out jumped an enormous, golden ape.

The ape landed on top of a man ahead of them who was standing with a net, and the ape stole his net and tied him up with it. All the men were quickly distracted by the ape, and as they were drawn into the commotion, the ape started to scream and tie all of the men up in their own nets. It was jumping, grabbing, sometimes picking up men and stuffing them inside any nets it was able to snatch, and Martin backed away and watched, as he began to see a pile assembling. A pile of men, all disarmed and tangled up in their own nets, a mass of squirming panic was beginning to build and the golden ape looked furious, hell-bent on making sure that every one of Jacobson's men was in its new collection, its new pile of dangerous men that it could be sure couldn't escape.

The Garganfan started helping, chasing men down through the woods as they ran away, grabbing them by the ankles and throwing them over towards the golden ape. The golden ape would catch the men, hook their feet or legs or arms in a piece of stolen net, and continue to build its pile. Soon every one of Jacobson's men in the forest had been captured, and the golden ape started to march back towards where Jacobson was.

The ape brought back Jacobson and his four initial guards, carrying them over its shoulders, and it added them to the pile. Jacobson seemed to have been completely demonstralised.

"Oh, what a lovely ape," Jacobson said, smiling slightly as the ape added him to the pile.

The Garganfan and the ape walked back and forth as they collected every fallen man that the Garganfan had already dealt with. The men were alive, unconscious, but were beginning to wake up as they were added to the ape's giant pile.

"What's happening?" one of the men said. "Stop! Help!"

Then the ape started to rub its hands together, and a flame emerged in its palms.

It looked at Martin, and said, in a very deep voice:

"Shall I end all of this?"

The ape knelt down, and held the flame close to the pile of men who were beginning to scream and plead for their lives.

"No! Wait, stop!" Martin said, running up to the ape. Part of him wanted the pile to be set ablaze. His mother was still lying on the floor behind them with a bleeding head.

"Um...Nerris...what shall we do?"

"Hahaha!" Nerris laughed, stooping down and picking up her Demonstraliser. "It's finally charged. Step aside, you lot."

The Garganfan was still stood on top of the pile of men, kicking at any of them who tried to escape. The Garganfan slid down the pile of men, backed away, and the golden ape, who was even taller than the Garganfan, backed away too as Martin did.

Martin watched Nerris as she aimed her Demonstraliser at the tangle of men squirming in the netted pile, all thinking they were about to be shot by a horrendous weapon. Martin turned to the golden ape and his focus switched to his mother.

"Can you heal people? Can you heal my mother?" Martin said to the ape.

"He can't," the Garganfan said. "But I know something that can. Let's go. She needs help, right now."

The Garganfan walked over and picked up Amanda in his arms. All of a sudden, the Garganfan was a caring, gentle creature that wasn't interested in fighting anything. As Martin looked back and saw that the golden ape was gone, he picked up the protective stone from the forest floor, and he shielded his eyes as the entire forest was lit up with the power of Nerris's Demonstraliser, shining over the pile of Jacobson and his men.

保
護

Protection

Chapter 13 - The Spirit Of Darkness

Kuyasaki, Myasako and Takashi were drinking tea in the corner of their dojo, where the mats ended and the ground was stony.

Myasako noticed that Kuyasaki's head darted towards the entrance of the dojo, where there stood an exhausted-looking Nayla, covered in dirt, with cuts on her face and arms.

Takashi stood and drew his sword.

"Yame!" Kuyasaki yelled at Takashi, meaning 'stop' in Japanese. Takashi stood, and didn't move.

Nayla was standing at the entrance, still panting slightly, looking straight at Kuyasaki.

"I escaped," she said. "I went to the fifth basement, like you said. I didn't even ask my father. I found my mother there, she was weak, tired and alone. I tried to break her out with me but when I was at the border of the compound she was snatched away from me. I had a choice, either to stay and be locked up like her, or to escape and come for help. I've come for your help."

Myasako noticed Takashi's hand was still gripped tightly around the handle of his sword, as if he was ready to swing it.

"You want to get her out of that place?" Kuyasaki said.

Nayla nodded.

Kuyasaki sat down.

"I don't believe you," he said.

Nayla's eyes twitched. She looked at Myasako. Myasako suddenly felt dreadful, as if he had let down his guard.

"Do you see how Senzi disregards your safety? He sent you here, alone, to try to capture Myasako again. We will not fight in this dojo. It is forbidden."

"What if I'm not alone?" Nayla smirked. "What if I *did* meet my mother after all, but she isn't as good as you think she is? What if that dark powerful spell over my mother's cellar was created by my mother, on purpose, to protect her from people like you?"

"Then that is not really your mother," Kuyasaki said. "Something else is living through her."

At that moment Myasako felt as if the entire country of Japan turned a shade darker. He saw his father stand up, grab the daggers from his waist, and Takashi crouched down low, holding the sword beside his head.

Myasako took out his nunchuks and saw everything turn into slow motion. He saw Nayla launch herself at his father, and his father kicked her so hard that she went flying out through the door.

As Nayla flew out, something else flew in, a dark, formless spirit that flew straight through Kuyasaki's body, straight through the swipe of Takashi's lethal sword, and Myasako felt himself grabbed by something from within. He felt hands grip around his heart, and he was lifted off the ground, without any control.

Suddenly everything sped up again, and Myasako was launched out of the dojo and shot up into the air. In the clutches of a dark spirit he was being carried far away from his home, beyond the Seishin Mountain, and toward a place he had never been.

*

The Garganfan was running with Martin's mother in his arms. She was still in a net. Her body had gone limp again.

"She's got some sort of brain injury," the Garganfan said. "Let's hope there's one somewhere nearby."

"What? What's nearby?" Martin said, running along, panicked and beginning to fear the worst.

"A Healybug," the Garganfan said, as if Martin should have known that already.

"A what?"

The Garganfan ignored Martin's question, and just kept running.

Eventually they came to a small meadow, full of golden-orange petals and flowers that were full of insects.

"Kneel down. Be quiet," the Garganfan said, placing Martin's mother on the ground and backing away slowly.

"Be more silent than anything that exists," the Garganfan said. "Imagine you don't exist for a moment."

Martin watched, quietly, at a mother that he felt powerless to help. He wanted healing powers, he wanted to be able to touch her and make her all better.

Martin looked to his side at the Garganfan. The Garganfan had eyes like bottomless pits. He had seen a thousand wars and fought millions of men to protect the forest that he loved, and Martin could see he had deep scars on his wooden, barky body.

"There!" the Garganfan said. But he didn't say it with his voice, he said it with his eyes. His beady dark eyes widened and pointed to a sight in the distance, and the noise of a very low, harmonious buzzing.

The buzzing noise grew louder and seemed to reverberate in every cell of Martin's body, making him feel lighter. In the distance he saw a red insect with a slight glow, travelling slowly towards them. It looked a bit like a large red beetle, and when it reached Martin's mother, it stopped and hovered.

Martin watched as the insect stopped in the air, seemed to inspect his mother in front of him, and then it darted straight into her slightly open mouth, disappearing from view.

Martin flinched and his instinct was to get that bug from out of his mother, but the Garganfan grabbed him and held his arms so tightly with his branchy fingers that Martin couldn't move an inch further.

"Just wait," the Garganfan whispered.

They could still hear the buzzing, but it was muffled, and after a few minutes of Martin's insides squirming, and the Garganfan watching with a very slight, wondrous smile, the Healybug popped out of his mother's mouth, and flew back into the meadow.

The Garganfan released his tight grip from around Martin's arms, and Martin ran towards his mum.

"Mum. Mum!"

She took a deep breath in, and with her eyes still closed, she smiled.

"Oh, my goodness," she said. She opened her eyes, and noticed she was covered in a huge net.

"Are we safe?" she said to Martin, beginning to remember what had just happened.

"Yes, Nerris is shooting all of them with her Demonstraliser," Martin said.

"And it worked?"

"It seemed to, yes. The Garganfan helped us too, and the Healybug helped you with your head."

"The what?" she said. "Are you being serious? I always assumed the Healybug was a myth..."

"It's real," the Garganfan said, as he approached the two of them. He kneeled down and began tearing open the net that still covered Amanda. She looked at him in amazement, and he kept speaking.

"In fact many stories of these creatures you may have heard about as a child, are true. There are many creatures in this forest that people think are only myths. Some are good, some are not so good, but many of them have very wise lessons to teach us. Others are just miracle workers."

133

Freed from her net, Amanda stood up through the gap the Garganfan had created, and they saw Nerris approach them in the distance.

"Can you believe it!" Nerris called. "It didn't kill them! It worked! The Demonstraliser works on humans!"

*

Myasako landed in the forest with a huge bump and a skid, and he was released by this dark energy, which materialised into a woman in front of him.

"You're mine now," the woman said. She was dressed in black, a thin Japanese woman wearing a black dress, with long dark nails that looked as if they had scratched many faces.

"Who are you?" Myasako said.

There was a pause, the woman looked confused.

"I'm...I'm...I work for Senzi. I'm his wife. I'm Nayla's mother. You are mine until Kuyasaki pays the ransom for your release. And if he doesn't pay, you will slowly be harmed, more and more until he is forced to release you."

Myasako felt an absolute absence of fear. There was something in him so strong that he found himself almost oblivious to any kind of negative outcome.

"I've heard about this forest," Myasako said. "This is the Shinwa Forest, isn't it? The forest where no one goes anymore?"

The woman said nothing.

"My father told me that I would be brought here when the time was right, when it was time for me to grow up and discover my true power."

"Well he was lying," the woman said. "Now stop talking. You are making me annoyed."

She flicked her wrist and Myasako flew back to become tied to a tree, a tree he couldn't move away from. He could feel ropes tied around his body, but he could see nothing around him.

"Where's Nayla?" Myasako asked.

"Stop talking!" the woman yelled. "She can look after herself."

Myasako looked at the ground. Then he looked up, and high up in the trees he could see a little monkey, looking down on what was happening.

The woman began to pace around, agitated.

"Are the stories true about this forest, what lives here?" Myasako asked.

"I don't know," the woman said. "Yes, they are. Especially all the bad ones."

"Have you been here before?"

The woman stopped pacing. She looked around. Her energy shifted, it became lighter again.

"Yes," she said. She had a different voice for a moment. Her face became lighter, as if a weight was lifted for a few seconds. Even her dress looked lighter.

"Yes, when I was younger," she said, "I was here, alone, I met a woman, a darkly-dressed woman and she offered me something..."

"What did she offer?" Myasako asked.

Suddenly the woman became dark again.

"Never mind! Shut up! You've said too much, now you will never speak again! I warned you about this!"

The woman pointed her finger at Myasako's mouth, and as a crackling green bolt erupted out of her finger, the monkey from above landed on her face.

The woman fell back, beginning to scream, and as she shifted into a pure, formless spirit, the monkey somehow clung on. The spirit was flying around the forest floor, trying to become free, but the monkey was clinging on for dear life until it started ripping away at the darkness. Myasako watched them as the invisible ropes around his body began to weaken, and the monkey began to scream. It was tearing through all darkness until it found a light at the bottom, and the light was so bright that it erupted out of the spirit and blew all the darkness away. It knocked the monkey back, on to the forest floor, and the monkey had to shield its eyes from the light as it climbed back up into the trees. Myasako closed his eyes too, covering them with his arms as they became free, and as the light dimmed again, Myasako looked and saw a different woman lying on the ground.

She was like the woman before, but much lighter – beautiful, angelic, even shining. He knew this was the woman that his father had been talking about, Nayla's mother before she was taken over by an evil spirit.

The woman stirred, sat up and blinked.

"Have you ever heard the story about the exorcist monkey?" Myasako said. "The monkey that likes to eat and tear through evil spirits? I think it just saved us from something very bad."

She looked around.

"Who are you?" she said.

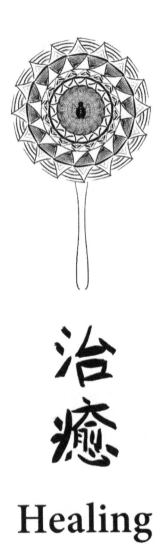

治
癒

Healing

Chapter 14 - Demonstralised

As Martin, his mother, Nerris and the Garganfan walked back through the forest, they saw the pile of men, still tangled up in nets.

"Excuse me?" someone said from the pile of men. It was Jacobson Muldridge, smiling at all of them. He had a bruised cheek from where the Garganfan had knocked him down.

"Excuse me, I'm sorry, but would you mind helping us get loose? We've become tied up somehow, me and my good employees. I was wondering, would you mind helping us?"

Martin looked into Jacobson's eyes. He had kind eyes, wealthy, infinite eyes that just wanted to do good.

"Who am I?" Martin said to him.

"Why, I believe your name is Martin," Jacobson said. "Have we met before? I remember I wanted something from you, I can't think what...we came here because...because I wanted something...I just can't remember what it was."

"Do you still want something from me?" Martin said.

"Oh, goodness no, nothing other than to be free from this net. No, I have plenty, what else could I possibly need? I just want to go home to my dear son, enjoy my life, that's all."

"Do you think it's permanent?" Martin whispered to Nerris.

Nerris looked at Jacobson.

"I have no idea," she said. "I hope it is. The Demonstraliser is designed to make biological changes that eradicate certain painful memories. I hope so, but I don't know. What I do fear is that if we leave them all here, trapped, it might create anger in some form, and it might start our problems all over again. Anyway, one man over there is starting to wriggle free."

One man had pulled out a small knife from his pocket, and was gradually cutting though the net.

"Let's release them," Nerris said, nodding to the Garganfan.

The Garganfan walked over, stared at Jacobson for a moment and then ripped open the net, just enough to let a few men out.

"If he ever causes trouble again, I will be forced to be far more harsh," the Garganfan said. "I will break bones, take lives, regardless of what any of you say. We Garganfans are bred to have compassion the first time, to try to teach rather than destroy. But if the same people approach with evil intent, we turn into monsters."

"Okay," Nerris said. "Thank you, my friend. Thank you for helping us."

The Garganfan nodded.

"Come back to see me," the Garganfan said to Martin. "We never had that fighting lesson in the end, did we?"

"No, we didn't," Martin said. "And if there's more – if there are more creatures to see, can you show me?"

"Yes," the Garganfan said. "but I can't guarantee it will always be safe. Mostly it is, but sometimes it's not. You might have to check with your mother first."

"Yes, he will," Martin's mother said. "We'll talk about it later. Let's just go home."

At that moment, they heard Jacobson's phone ring. Jacobson was clambering out of the net, and he picked up the phone.

"Hello? Yes, yes fine thanks. Stone? What stone? I don't know what you're talking about..."

Martin touched the stone through his pocket.

"Well if it's his, it's his...well that doesn't make any sense, does it? No, no I don't want it. No. I said no. Yes, pick us up please, you can see where we are."

He hung up the phone.

"Now," he said, "what are you fine people doing for dinner...and I'm sorry, what are you?"

"I'm a Garganfan."

"What are you fine people, and Garganfan, doing for dinner? Would you like to come round to my house?"

"No thanks," Martin's mother said quickly. "We have to go."

"Very well," Jacobson said. "Take care now!"

Martin, the Garganfan, his mother and Nerris walked away, and Martin looked back to see Jacobson waving, as if he was a completely different man.

"I hope it's permanent," Martin said.

"If it's not, just bring him to me," the Garganfan said. "Good evening to you all." The Garganfan started clambering up the nearest tree to rest in the canopy above.

"Goodbye, and thank you!" Martin called. "Thank you for saving us!"

The Garganfan paused at the top of the tree, turned to look at Martin, and nodded. Then he disappeared into the branches.

Freedom

Chapter 15 - The Navigation Troll

Nayla had run off into the distance, away from the dojo. Her orders were to allow her mother to capture Myasako, and that had been done. Kuyasaki watched her as she ran, and he decided to follow her.

"Stay here," Kuyasaki said to Takashi. "Guard the dojo in case any more come."

Takashi stood at the entrance of the dojo, completely still, holding his sword as if he was a statue made of stone.

Kuyasaki tracked Nayla. He hid behind vans and trailers and small buildings as she continued to run down the road.

After a few minutes, when they were on an open expanse of road, where the town had ended, he saw Nayla stop.

The road was empty. It was as if something distracted her. Kuyasaki felt the force of invisibility begin to take him over involuntarily, but as Nayla turned around, it was as if her entire demeanour shifted to become lighter. There had been a dark force ruling over her for quite some time, and now it was gone.

She sat down on the side of the road. Kuyasaki walked out from behind a small car, completely visible, and he approached her.

"Something has left me," she said. "What I did, what I was doing...I'm sorry. Something had a hold of me."

Kuyasaki walked up to her.

"It's okay," he said. "It seems as if the darkness that took over your mother had also infected you. But now that darkness might be gone. Wherever Myasako is, he may have witnessed some kind of exorcism, a removal of the dark spirit."

Nayla stood up and looked around.

"Everything looks lighter," she said. "I always knew my father was a bad man, but it never seemed to matter. Now I don't want to work for him as long as he continues to do bad things."

She looked around again.

"But I have nowhere to go. All I've ever known is the inside of that compound. This is the only time I've ever been let out."

"We have room above the dojo," Kuyasaki said. "You can stay with us, train with us, and develop your skills for the good of all. You might even be able to help your father see the light too."

"Thank you," Nayla said. "Thank you. I feel so tired."

"Then sleep. We have a spare bed."

"Thank you," she said again. "What about Myasako? My mother?" she said, remembering what had happened. "Where did they go? Are they okay?"

"I am quite sure that they are fine. Myasako is well trained. He will find himself doing things, asking things, suggesting things that he doesn't even realise will benefit the situation. Wherever he has been taken to will only develop his skills, and he may have helped to liberate your mother from whatever was living through her. I feel that we will see them both very soon."

Uncle Kuyasaki and his liberated niece began walking back to the dojo, where Takashi was still waiting, as motionless as stone.

*

When Jacobson Muldridge arrived home, his son Arthur was eating a bowlful of sweets. He was eating them like cereal while watching the television. When he saw his father walk into his room, he almost stopped chewing.

"Dad!" he said. He still had a mouthful of sweets. "Dad, what happened, did you get the stone?"

"No. Come with me, Arthur. We need to take a walk together, outside. It's such a lovely day."

Arthur looked stunned, and actually stopped chewing. His father had never asked anything like this before.

"No way!" Arthur said. "I've already had to walk up and down the stairs twice because the maid forgot to bring me my spoon! No way am I walking."

"Either you come with me, or I carry you out like a baby," Jacobson said.

"You couldn't. I'm too big and strong," said Arthur. "And what's happened to your face? Have you been punched?"

Jacobson walked over to the television, and turned it off. Then he took the bowl of sweets from the tight grip of Arthur's hands.

"Come on. You need some fresh air, and a cleansing of your mind. I seem to have had one. You need one too."

And with a reluctant yell of frustration, Arthur followed his father out of his room, with a sudden feeling of joy that his father actually wanted to do something with him for once.

*

Myasako was in the woods, with the woman who was technically his aunt. Her name was Shieng.

"Where do we go now?" Shieng asked. "I can't even remember where I live, or how to get out of the forest."

Myasako wasn't sure what to do. His father's voice rang in his ears:

"If you don't know what to do, that's okay. Just be quiet, let it be, and an answer will come."

Myasako looked around, and he had a vision pop up in his mind, something he used to read about in a book called Mythical Creatures Of The Forest. The book had one chapter about a creature called a Navigation Troll.

"I have an idea, but I don't know if it will work," Myasako said.

"What?" said Shieng.

"Give me your hand," Myasako said. "Then touch that tree behind you."

She did as he said, and with his free hand, Myasako touched another tree close by.

"Now," Myasako said. "Now you have to imagine a bad memory that still lives inside you, one that you don't like but still seems to pester you. Can you think of one?"

"Yes, I can," Shieng said. She was thinking of the day when she met the evil spirit in the forest, and it offered to keep her family safe forever in return for a favour.

"Okay," Myasako said. "I can too." Myasako remembered the time he saw Martin's mother poisoned and threatened at the hands of Jacobson Muldridge.

"Now," said Myasako. "You have to be willing to give up this bad memory. You have to say, 'I give this memory to the Navigation Troll'."

"I give this memory to the Navigation Troll," Shieng said.

"I give this memory to the Navigation Troll," Myasako said, and suddenly there was a grumbling, a rumbling, and out of the earth in front of them emerged a sleepy, weary-looking troll who looked like it had been sleeping for thousands of years.

It yawned as it emerged, and the rumbling from the ground slowed down and stopped.

"Ah," it said. "I haven't been needed for...for a very long time. What will it be? Where do you want to go?"

"Back to my home," Myasako said, "the dojo in the town beyond the Seishin Mountain."

"Me too," Shieng said. "I'm too afraid of what will happen if I go back to Senzi," she said to Myasako. "Before I met that dark spirit, Senzi was getting himself into trouble. He parted ways with your father and became interested in terrible ways to make money. I disagreed with him at every turn, and one day I woke up here, in the forest, and was confronted by that dark woman."

"Well, it's obvious the baggage you are carrying," the Navigation Troll said to her, pulling out a notepad and a pencil from somewhere. "That one ought to be powerful enough to take you both to where you need to be. But what about you, lad, want to pay any extra? It might make your journey a bit smoother."

"Yes," Myasako said. "I have one."

The Navigation Troll peered into Myasako's eyes and detected the memory. Painful memories contained precious energy that the troll used to transport people. It squinted for a while, then began writing something else down.

"Yes, very good, very good," it said. "Okay then, now this will feel strange. All you have to do is touch my hair. Then I will take you to your dojo, in return for both of these painful memories. Okay?"

"Okay," they both said.

"Touch the hair then, touch the hair!" the troll said, becoming slightly impatient.

His hair looked long and dirty and scraggly, but as soon as Myasako touched it, it felt like silk, and as Shieng touched the hair too, they were evaporated into thin air, and they could see the faint outline of the Navigation Troll, running through some kind of portal in an unseen part of the universe, and they were being whisked back to the safety of Myasako's home.

運送する

Transport

Chapter 16 - To Adventure

When Martin, Nerris and his mother arrived back at Nerris's house, they all just went and sat down. There was a while where no one said anything. They were all just staring into space.

Then Nerris snapped out of it.

"Drinks?" Nerris said, ready to stand.

"I'll get them," said Martin, going into the kitchen.

"So what you gonna do?" Nerris said quietly to her sister. "You gonna take Martin back to his normal life, or will you let him explore what's really out there in the forest, let him see what no one believes to be real?"

Martin's mother looked uncomfortable.

"I don't know," she said. "I can see him growing into a powerful young man, but all I want to do is keep him safe."

Martin walked back in carrying glasses of water. Nerris had some kind of contraption that made the water re-energise you completely after drinking. It was as if you had just had a good night's sleep.

"Thanks Martin," Nerris said, taking a drink.

"And what do you want to do, boy?" she said to Martin. "You've still got a few weeks' holiday left."

"I want to go back into the forest and learn more from the Garganfan," said Martin. "That's all I want to do. Can we stay here any longer, Nerris? Mum?"

"You can stay here as long as you like," Nerris said, looking at his mother.

"Okay, we can stay a bit longer," Martin's mother said, "but we aren't doing anything dangerous, you'll only meet good creatures in the forest, if any. Not bad ones."

Nerris smiled.

"Here's to adventure," Nerris said, raising her glass.

"To adventure," Martin said, doing the same.

"To adventure," Martin's mother said, holding her glass up slightly shakily.

*

After Martin had been sitting with his aunt and mother, drinking the rejuvenating water and discussing what had been going on during the past few days, Martin noticed something.

He had a habit of every now and again checking that the stone was still in his pocket by pressing against his trouser leg. He realised he hadn't checked since they left Jacobson in the forest, and as he went to check, his heart lurched.

He couldn't feel the stone. He put his drinking glass on the table in front of him, stood, and started patting himself down.

"It's gone," he said. "The stone. I've lost it."

"Well where else have you been?" his mother asked, sitting up.

"Nowhere...just the kitchen," Martin said, running out and going into the kitchen, getting on his hands and knees and looking into every corner of the room.

His mother was checking down the back of the sofa. She could normally find anything that Martin lost, but she couldn't find the stone.

As Martin rushed back in, feeling his heart rate steadily increasing, he saw Nerris stand up and walk towards the basement.

"Where are you going?" Martin said, crawling on the floor to look under the sofas.

"Hang on," Nerris said, and soon she reappeared from the basement, holding a small hand-held device with a screen and a small antenna on it.

"This is something else I've been working on. It's the lost item detector. It's based on Ganonites."

Martin stared at her blankly.

"Every lost item gives off a signal if it wants to be found," she continued. "The signal consists of particles that I like to call Ganonites, and these Ganonites have no limit to their range of detection."

She was pushing buttons on the device, and Martin could hear a very faint whirring sound.

"Look," she said, pointing at the screen. "These are all the lost items in the nearby area, all giving off signals that they want to be found by the owner."

Martin looked at the screen. It had a map of the area, including the houses outlined with faint blue lines. He could see lots of green blobs of varying intensities, often sitting within houses.

"The brightness of the blobs usually indicates how recently they have been lost," Nerris said. "Recently lost items are hungry to be found, giving off a far greater density of Ganonites compared to those that have been lost for years."

"Well how do we know which is the stone?" Martin said, looking at all the green blobs.

"We don't, we don't know," she said, "but..."

Nerris made the screen zoom out so that it included the forest. She zoomed out even further, and they could see the brightest green blob of them all, shining out from inside the forest.

"There!" Martin said. "What's that?"

Nerris zoomed in on the brightest green blob, and it was on the move. It was being carried by something, in between the trees.

"I think that's your stone," Nerris said. "Something has taken it."

*

When Myasako arrived just behind the dojo with his aunt Shieng, he looked around for the Navigation Troll, but couldn't see him.

"Where is he?" Myasako whispered. He had read about the Navigation Troll saying goodbye at the destination and making sure his clients were happy, but for some reason, he was nowhere to be seen.

Myasako felt lighter than before, a darkness had left him. Shieng felt a great liberation, as if her body was singing with joy. She knew that a darkness had taken her over in the past, but the trauma and pain had been removed from her memory. She almost felt reborn.

Before they even began walking, Kuyasaki appeared in front of them.

"Kuyasaki?" Shieng said.

"Shieng, hello," Kuyasaki said, smiling.

Shieng ran up to Kuyasaki, they embraced and Myasako followed after.

"It's good to see you, son," Kuyasaki said.

Myasako bowed.

"Come," Kuyasaki said, leading them both inside the dojo. "There's someone you will want to meet, properly, if she's not yet gone to sleep."

*

As the Garganfan found a comfortable spot high up in the trees, he looked down one last time at the forest. He could see Jacobson being lifted out of the forest by a quiet, hovering machine with other men in it. He could see other men who had previously come with bad intentions, now leaving the forest quietly and peacefully. And then everything became very silent, just as the Garganfan was drifting off to sleep, he noticed something very strange. He was sure, very sure that he could see something hovering in mid-air, being carried along the forest floor. He peered closer with his beady eyes, leaned forward, and saw that it was a stone, a small grey stone that Martin had pulled out of his pocket, the stone that the Garganfan recognised from somewhere deep in his memory, somewhere that he could not place.

Something told him he must move, that he must not let the stone out of his sight, and so he sat up in the branches, and began to follow this floating stone, as he glided across the trees.

*

As Jacobson and his son, Arthur, walked around the grounds of his large estate, they approached a wooded area. "I love you, Arthur," Jacobson suddenly said.

At first Arthur felt sick, as if his insides were rebelling against such a thing. Then the rebellion ceased, and Arthur felt a warmth that he had never felt before.

"Really?" Arthur said. "Do you really?"

"Yes," Jacobson said. "I do. I might have never said it before, but I do."

Arthur felt as if a part of himself that had been missing for a long time was placed back inside his heart. The air smelt fresher, he felt lighter on his feet. He felt far less angry, even happy, for once.

And then, as the two entered the woodland on Jacobson's private land, they heard a panting noise.

Arthur looked to his left and saw a stone floating in mid-air.

"Dad, what's that?"

Jacobson looked, and as the stone approached, a body formed around the stone. It was a grey, hunched-over creature that looked like a gargoyle, but it had very large feet and a very hunched back.

"Your lordship," the creature said, bowing and presenting Jacobson with the stone.

"What's this? And what are you?" Jacobson said. Arthur was hiding behind him. The creature looked evil.

"The stone, as requested, your lordship," the creature said again. Arthur noticed a slight smile began to creep onto its face.

"What did I request?" Jacobson said, struggling to remember the mind he used to have.

"You requested the protective stone, if anything were to go wrong. I watched the whole thing, your lordship. You were blasted with something,

something that took your thieving intents away, so I snuck up behind the boy, the boy with the stone, and I removed it from his pocket while he was speaking to those other two women. I waited until that wooden creature went up into the trees."

"I...well I'm sorry," Jacobson said, "I don't want it. We must return it at once to the owner."

"No no, your lordship," the creature said. "We had a deal. We made a deal, your lordship, you remember. The oath was made. You said you would give anything for that stone, anything. Anything on your land, I could have, you said. And I have made my choice. Here is the stone."

The creature dropped it at Jacobson's feet.

"And in return, I will take your son."

"No," Jacobson said. "No, not my son. No, he's been ill-behaved, I know, but that will soon be fixed. It's my fault, I never paid him any..."

"He's mine now," the creature said, and in a flash, the creature disappeared again, and Arthur was snatched off his feet.

"Dad!" Arthur yelled. He was being dragged away quickly, quicker than any animal could run. "Dad! Dad help!"

Leaves were flying up around Arthur's hands as he tried to claw his way back to his father.

"Arthur!" Jacobson yelled, sprinting, trying to catch up, but Arthur was gone, and Jacobson was left alone.

As the Garganfan watched this happen from the trees above, he saw Jacobson kneel down, pick up the stone, and carry it away towards his house.

"Oi," the Garganfan said, jumping down from the trees and landing on the ground. "That stone is not yours."

Jacobson turned around.

"I know," Jacobson said. "I know it's not. I'm going to return it to Martin."

"I'll do it," the Garganfan said, still suspicious of Jacobson and his plans. "Give it to me. I'll return it."

Jacobson threw the stone towards the Garganfan, who caught it with one hand. As soon as the Garganfan touched the stone, he felt a power surge through him that he had never felt before. He felt as if he had the power of a thousand creatures coursing through his entire body, as if he could fight with the ferocity of an entire army of Garganfans.

"My son, Arthur. Can you help get him back?" Jacobson said.

The Garganfan was having trouble dealing with the amount of power he could feel. He needed an outlet for it. He could smell things, see things and hear things that he had never been able to sense before. He could see that there was no more evil in Jacobson, just a terrible guilt and sense of hopelessness, with thoughts of Arthur being eaten alive, or tortured.

"I will help," the Garganfan said. "Wait here."

The Garganfan exploded into the distance, where he could still hear the panting and running of this gargoyle-like creature, and the screams of Arthur, that were far off amongst the trees.

*

In the evening, Myasako was eating a meal with Takashi, Nayla, his newly found aunt Shieng, and his father, Kuyasaki.

"How did you feel inside that forest?" Kuyasaki asked him.

"I felt strangely fearless," Myasako said, "as if there was a power there that was able to take care of me."

"You will return to that forest for more training," Kuyasaki said. "In the coming weeks we will return to the Seishin Mountain, where there are more tasks for you to perform and places to visit. Absorbing the wisdom of the forest, making your way through its challenges, meeting its many inhabitants, will be one aspect of this."

Myasako looked down into his food, and realised that there was never an end-point. His training would continue until the day he died.

"But tonight, and for the next few days, everyone here has earnt a good rest," Kuyasaki said, noticing that Myasako looked slightly disheartened.

"We will enjoy our time together, learn from each other, and enjoy the gifts of nature."

"What about Senzi?" Shieng said. "What if he comes back for us, what if he uses everything he has to try to get me and Nayla back?"

"Don't worry about that," Kuyasaki said. "We will hear him coming."

Family

Chapter 17 - The Possession

"Look at it now!" Martin said, looking at the shining green blob on Nerris's lost item detector. "Now it's moving even faster, and in the opposite direction."

"This is strange," said Nerris, "I've never seen anything moving so quickly."

"We have to get it back," Martin said.

"No, Martin," his mother said. "It's far too dangerous."

"But Mum," Martin said, "I'm still the owner of the stone. I haven't given it away. So if I'm near it, it will protect me from any harm."

"That might be right, but it might be wrong," Nerris said. "The stone might not think like that. How do you know it's still really yours? Maybe it's looking to be with someone else..."

Martin didn't like the question. Without the stone, he felt as if he was missing part of himself. His mother could see how troubled he looked, and she sighed, with her head in her hands.

"I just want everything to be normal again," she said, looking at the floor. "I should have never let you go to Japan in the first place, Martin. Everything was normal back then."

"But I was getting bullied," Martin said. "Remember? But now if Arthur tries to bully me again, with or without a stone, I won't let him. I won't let him bully me any more."

Martin and Nerris noticed that the glowing green light on the screen had stopped. It wasn't moving.

"It's not too far away now is it, Nerris? Five minutes in?" Martin said.

"Maybe more," Nerris said. "It's not wise to go that deep without someone like the Garganfan to protect you."

"Then let's go and find the Garganfan," Martin said. "We have to get the stone back."

Nerris looked at him. She noticed he looked panicked. "Why?" Nerris said.

"Because...because it's mine," Martin said.

"And why else?"

"Because...because it will keep us safe. It will always keep us safe. It will keep me safe, or I can give it to Mum and it will keep her safe."

Martin was starting to fidget. The stone meant he could feel safe again. Without it, he felt on edge, vulnerable.

"I think with something like this," Nerris said, "if it's meant to come back to you, it will. By itself. I think you've grown too attached to it. Now you're dependent on it, maybe even scared to be without it?"

"That's not true!" Martin said angrily. "No. It was a gift. A gift from Kuyasaki and I've let him down. I said I would look after it, and I've failed."

"What would Kuyasaki say about all of this?" Martin's mother asked, looking up from her seat.

Martin wondered what Kuyasaki would say. He saw Kuyasaki in his mind. There was a pause.

"Calm down," Martin said. "He'd tell me to calm down and become my own fortress, rather than depending on something else all the time. He would say there are no accidents, and not to blame myself."

For a moment, Martin felt relieved at this advice. He enjoyed a moment of freedom. But then a hunger for getting that stone back arose in him even more strongly. If he could just get the stone back, and never let it out of his sight ever again, then he would be able to relax. He and his mother would always be safe.

"We'll go back to the forest tomorrow," Nerris said. "We'll visit the Garganfan and see what he has to say. He might have seen what happened. It's starting to get dark now anyway, and it's never a good idea to go near the forest when it's dark."

"But what about the Ganonites it's giving off?" Martin said. "The stone wants to be found! You said so yourself, we can't just leave it."

"You heard her, Martin," his mother said. "It's not safe when it's dark. The stone will have to wait."

Martin's mother stood up, and as Nerris left to make the evening meal, Martin secretly wondered if he should sneak out at night, all by himself.

*

That night, Amanda had a terrible dream. Martin had snuck out of the house, almost possessed by a blind desire to get back his lost stone. He had a feeling in him that he would not be complete without it, and that if he just got the stone back, everything would be fine, forever. She could see him walking through the streets with Nerris's lost item detector, and he disappeared into the darkness of the woods. And as he disappeared, something landed on him. Something with legs.

She burst awake with fear. She got up out of bed and ran to Martin's room.

"No!" she screamed.

Nerris trundled in, squinty-eyed and dazed.

"What?" Nerris said "What is it?"

"He's gone," Amanda said. "He's left a note."

She handed the note to Nerris, and Nerris read the note:

"Gone to get my stone back."

終わり

The End

Book 3 out now...

Continue The Adventure!

Find out what happens to Martin when he risks everything to try to retrieve the lost protective stone, and join Nayla and Myasako as they undergo the next stage of ninja training in the Shinwa Forest...

Book 3 available now on Amazon.

Get the full 6-book series on Amazon now, and join the adventures of Martin, Myasako and Nayla...

Out Now On Amazon:

Coming Soon:

Also By Adam For Ages 8+

Fred: The Creature Sent To Save Us All

Happiness Is Inside: 25 Inspirational Stories For Greater Peace Of Mind

Mythical Creatures Of The Forest
For more adventures with the Garganfan, the Navigation Troll, the Healybug and many others...

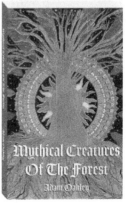

*If you enjoyed this book, **please leave a review on Amazon** – it helps the book to reach more people!*

Thank you.

Follow Adam on social media here:

@ninjakidsbook

@adamoakleybooks

About The Author

Adam is not yet a fully-fledged ninja with powers of teleportation or invisibility, but maybe one day he will be.

For now he is happy doing kickboxing, wrestling and Brazilian jiu jitsu during the week, in between growing organic food, writing, and spending time with his family.

He hopes you loved reading the book, and he is grateful for any young readers or parents who can leave a review on Amazon to help the book reach more people.

He thanks you for your support, and is always available to contact via one of his websites:

www.InnerPeaceNow.com

www.AdamOakleyBooks.com